"Yes?"

Phoebe looked up[...] fell on the man in the doorway. The *tall, blond, brown-eyed man* who sent a charge through her body the likes of which she'd never felt before. She tried to remember why she was there, to force words—coherent or otherwise—through her gaping mouth, but she could focus on nothing other than the man standing in front of her.

"Can I help you?"

His voice was rugged yet kind as his gaze slid across the baby and made its way slowly down Phoebe's body, making her wish she'd done more than pull her long hair into a ponytail and run a swath of gloss across her lips. He seemed to hesitate slightly on her attire, his right eyebrow inching upward as he zeroed in on her paint-spattered shirt.

"I'm here to deliver this—" she raised the envelope "—to Tate Williams. Is he home?"

The man's mouth widened into a slight smile as he leaned against the door frame, the noon sun picking out flecks of amber amid the soft brown of his eyes. "Maybe."

Dear Reader,

Love sought is good, but given unsought is better.

I love that quote from William Shakespeare.
It's beautiful, it's poignant and—in the case of
Kayla's Daddy—it's dead-on.

You see, prior to this book, I was a cozy mystery
writer. Which means I crafted a story around a
crime. So when the notion of a misplaced letter first
came to me, I assumed I'd turn it into a mystery. It's
what I did with ideas.

Fortunately for me, the story had other ideas.

Kayla's Daddy is the first romance I've ever written.
It's also the book I'm most proud of to date. First
and foremost it's about love—the kind of love that's
meant to be…the kind of love that's oblivious to
money, background, health and age…the kind of
love that catches you in its grip when you least
expect it.

But it's also about taking a chance. For Tate,
for Phoebe, for Bart and for the residents of
Quinton Lane.

And finally, it's about you taking a chance on me.
I hope you'll love this story and these characters as
much as I do.

Best wishes,

Laura Bradford

Kayla's Daddy
LAURA BRADFORD

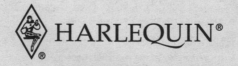

HARLEQUIN®

TORONTO • NEW YORK • LONDON
AMSTERDAM • PARIS • SYDNEY • HAMBURG
STOCKHOLM • ATHENS • TOKYO • MILAN • MADRID
PRAGUE • WARSAW • BUDAPEST • AUCKLAND

Recycling programs
for this product may
not exist in your area.

ISBN-13: 978-0-373-75293-5

KAYLA'S DADDY

Copyright © 2010 by Laura Bradford.

www.eHarlequin.com

Printed in U.S.A.

ABOUT THE AUTHOR

Since the age of ten, Laura Bradford hasn't wanted to do anything other than write—news articles, feature stories, business copy and whatever else she could come up with to pay the bills. But they were always diversions from the one thing she wanted to write most...fiction.

Today, with an Agatha Award nomination under her belt and a new mystery series with Berkley Prime Crime, Laura is thrilled to have crossed into the romance genre with her all-time favorite series, Harlequin American Romance.

When she's not writing, Laura enjoys reading, hiking, traveling and all things chocolate. She lives in New York with her two daughters. To contact her, visit her Web site, www.laurabradford.com.

For Jim

Chapter One

Phoebe Jennings glanced at the envelope on the empty passenger seat, her gaze lingering on the flowery penmanship and faded postmark from nearly four decades ago. Its delayed delivery was explained by a polite, yet formal, note of apology attached to it by a rubber band.

Only it wasn't *her* letter. Just her address.

A blaring horn forced her to look up, to focus on the road and the line of cars that had heeded the green light the moment it changed. Was she crazy, driving to the other side of Cedarville to deliver a letter to someone she'd never met?

Especially when she could have simply given it back to the post office?

Probably.

Then again, if she didn't deliver it herself, curiosity would eat at her day and night, making it difficult to finish the Dolangers' portrait by Friday. Blowing that deadline was out of the question if she was going to make next month's rent.

And feed Kayla.

Peeking into the rearview mirror, Phoebe smiled at

the child sleeping in the forward-facing car seat, the side of her heart-shaped face snuggled against a tiny pillow. Finishing the painting was the difference between interrupted and uninterrupted time with Kayla. It was the difference between restless nights and sleeping peacefully. And it was the first step in teaching her daughter the satisfaction that comes from working toward a dream.

Though, in all fairness, job satisfaction probably didn't fall terribly high on Kayla's list of priorities. Those spots were reserved for special things like Cheerios and Elmo.

As it should be.

With her eyes back on the road, Phoebe slowed as she approached Twilight Drive, the homes getting bigger and more ostentatious the farther into West Cedarville she drove. The view from her window wasn't a surprise; she'd known what to expect. Yet somehow the wealth that suddenly surrounded her brought a pang she hadn't expected.

This drive was an unwanted trip down memory lane—one littered with jagged life lessons, mammoth-size potholes and an occasional round of second-guessing.

Shaking her head, Phoebe willed herself to focus on the moment, to leave the past where it belonged. At least *her* past, anyway.

Tate Williams's past was another thing entirely.

From the moment she'd pulled the letter from her mailbox that morning, her thoughts had traveled to the ends of the earth in pursuit of a story worthy of such an old correspondence. The lone clue she had to the possible nature of the letter came from its army post office address, one that had long since expired. The forty-year-old postmark suggested it could have been meant for a soldier in Vietnam.

Had Tate Williams been sent a letter from a friend? Had someone been trying to give him news from home? Or had a stateside classroom initiated contact with the soldier as part of a writing assignment?

Phoebe could only guess. And guess she had. Over and over again.

But no more.

Brushing an errant strand of hair from her face, she pulled to a stop at 14 Starry Night Drive, her stomach churning ever so slightly. Judging by the time of day— noon—and the looks of the house, she'd bet good money she would be greeted by a maid or a cook. Maybe even a butler.

None of whom would be her first choice.

Sure, Mrs. Applewhite's description of Tate Williams hadn't been terribly flattering, but handing a decades-old letter to its rightful owner was worth tangling with a lion, right? Besides, Phoebe knew better than to put too much stock in her elderly next-door neighbor's assessment of people.

"Full of himself, that's what Tate Williams was. Too good for the likes of any of us. Good riddance, I say. And it will do you well to stay away from him…you mark my words, Phoebe Jennings."

Looking at the postmark one last time, Phoebe clasped the envelope and stepped from the car, her neighbor's words of caution falling away as she opened the back door and pulled a still-sleeping Kayla into her arms.

"So much for Mommy's exciting adventure, huh?"

Phoebe whispered into her daughter's ear as she cuddled her against her shoulder and moved toward the front door.

Everything about the outside of the home exuded the sterility of wealth. Professionally manicured bushes interspersed with glass-and-copper luminaries lined the stone walkway. The colorless landscaping served as a perfect accompaniment to the brick exterior of the home, the only offset coming from the two-story, white pillared entrance.

What was it about color that made the rich balk? Was it the rejection of individuality? Or the fear of the unknown?

Probably a little bit of both. Though she'd never understand how an aversion to change could breed success.

She gently patted Kayla's bottom and took a slow, deep breath. All morning she'd imagined this moment, envisioned the excited smile on the face of Tate Williams as he was reunited with a piece of his past. Now that she was finally here, she could hardly wait to see how her image meshed with reality.

"Here we go, Kayla," she whispered. Spying a small white button to the left of the door, Phoebe pressed it and waited. The melodic sound of a bell wafted through the closed panel in a clear summons. With no response.

She'd considered the possibility someone else would answer, even planned how she'd go about hanging on to the letter until she could meet the addressee face-to-face. But no answer at all? Her mind hadn't even begun to figure *that* one out.

Fortunately, it didn't matter. Because as she was mentally reviewing the contents of her glove compartment in the hopes of finding paper and a pen, the door opened.

"Yes?"

Phoebe looked up, all thoughts of pen, paper and mail delivery gone as her gaze fell on the man in the doorway. The tall, blond, brown-eyed man who sent a charge through her body the likes of which she'd never felt before. She tried to remember why she was there, to force words—coherent or otherwise—through her gaping mouth, but she could focus on nothing other than the gorgeous man standing in front of her, casually dressed in khaki slacks and a white, button-down shirt open at the neck.

"Can I help you?"

His voice was kind as his gaze slid across the baby and then slowly down Phoebe's body, making her wish she'd done more than pull her long hair into a ponytail and swipe some gloss across her lips. He seemed to hesitate slightly on her attire, his right eyebrow inching upward as he zeroed in on her paint-spattered shirt.

In an instant his demeanor changed, his expression switching from curious to deer-in-the-headlights. "Look, I don't need any work done. I just had the interior painted about six months ago and—"

She felt her eyebrow cock upward as a string of biting comebacks zipped through her mind. But she resisted. Ignorance was ignorance, as her grandmother used to say. It knew no boundaries—monetary or otherwise. And if two years of loving someone hadn't been enough to correct misperceptions, a two-minute conversation between strangers didn't have a prayer. And besides, Kayla didn't need to be woken to clipped words and icy stares.

"I'm not here to paint your walls. I'm here to deliver

this—" she raised the envelope, her voice void of its normal happy lilt "—to Tate Williams. Is he home?"

The man's mouth widened in a slight smile as he leaned against the door frame, the noon sun picking out flecks of amber amid the soft brown of his eyes. "Maybe."

Any lingering doubt that wealth and infuriation went hand in hand was virtually gone. As was her window of opportunity, judging by the way Kayla's body stiffened against Phoebe's shoulder.

She quickly glanced down at her watch. "I hate to be rude, but I only have a little time. The day job calls and—"

"Looks to me like the day job is sleeping." He smiled at the baby and tiny creases formed beside his eyes.

She stared at him, her hand reaching to pat Kayla's back. "She's not a *job*. She's my daughter. There's a big differ—"

He pushed himself off the door frame and rested his arms across his muscular chest, the fabric of his shirt pulling taut in the process. Phoebe swallowed and looked away.

Granted, it had been a while since she'd been with a man, but the desire to feel those arms around her body was nothing short of shocking. Ludicrous, really. Men like Tate Williams weren't interested in women like her. She knew that. Had lived through the painful proof firsthand.

But still. He was gorgeous....

"Look, is Tate Williams available to speak to me or should I just come back later?"

"Who's asking?"

Kayla's head popped up and looked around, her tiny

hand pinching Phoebe's chin as her gaze came to rest on Mr. Infuriating. He winked at her.

Phoebe gulped. "I am."

His eyes remained on the baby even as his words were directed at her. "I realize *you're* asking, I'm standing right here. What I'm trying to find out is your name. You do have one of those, right?"

She felt her cheeks warm, her palms moisten. Served her right for thinking like a lust-struck teenager. "Oh. Sorry. I'm Phoebe. Phoebe Jennings." She moved the letter to her left hand and stuck out her right. "Could I—"

"And?" He pointed at Kayla.

"And what?" This man was seriously driving her loony. So much for trying to do a good deed.

"Who's *this* little beauty?"

She looked down at her daughter, the tension in her body easing momentarily. "I'm sorry. This is Kayla. Anyway, could I speak with Mr. Williams now, please?"

"Absolutely."

The man didn't budge. He simply continued to stand there, alternating between making faces at the baby and grinning at Phoebe. Was this the way he treated everyone?

"Am I missing something?" she asked through clenched teeth.

"Just the part about actually handing over the envelope." He reached out, his palm upward. "It's a good thing you're a painter instead of a mailman because you wouldn't keep your job long."

The meaning of his words finally registered. "*You're* Tate Williams?"

He nodded, his mischievous smile lighting his face.

"But you can't be." Phoebe looked down at the envelope in her hand. "You're too young. Way too young."

"Excuse me?"

She knew she sounded like an idiot, but she didn't care. She'd done the math. Even if Tate Williams had been a young child when the letter was mailed, he'd have to be in his midforties by now. The man standing in front of her was thirty-three at best.

Phoebe stammered for an explanation that sounded semi-intelligent even to her own ears. "This letter was postmarked nearly forty years ago. There's no way—" she motioned toward him "—this could be for you."

"Let me see that."

He stepped outside and reached for her hand, his grip gentle yet strong. She shivered as his breath grazed her cheek, sending her thoughts racing, only to be pulled back to the present by a grunt.

"Oh. I see now. It's for Tate Williams, all right. Just not *this* Tate Williams." He released her and returned to the doorway, his playful nature all but gone. "The Tate Williams you're looking for doesn't live here. I'm sorry."

"But—but you do know him, right?"

The man gripped the edge of the door as if to close it. "Yeah, I know him."

She looked down at the envelope, the stories she'd attributed to the misplaced letter rushing her thoughts once again. "Do you know how I could find this other Tate Williams? Or better yet, could you help me get this to him?"

A cloud passed over the man's face and his words became more clipped. "No. I can't."

Can't or won't? She suspected there was quite a difference.

She tried another approach. "I feel sort of obligated to make sure he gets it. It could be important."

The man's eyes narrowed as he looked at her. "If it hasn't been missed in nearly forty years, I doubt it's important."

"But still—"

"Look, Mrs. Jen—"

"Miss. *Miss* Jennings. I mean, Phoebe."

His expression softened briefly, his words still short and clipped. "Okay. Phoebe. Why do you care so much? And how, may I ask, did you end up with the letter in the first place?"

Normally, she would have resented the questions from a man so unwilling to answer hers. But if it helped get the information she wanted...

"I live *here*—" she reached across Kayla's back and pointed to the label that had been placed alongside the original address "—and so it showed up in my mailbox."

"You live at 2565 Quinton Lane?"

She nodded, shifting Kayla from one arm to the other. "I moved in about six months ago. No sign of any previous owners until this morning." She raised the envelope into the air and blew at a strand of hair that had escaped her scrunchie. "I asked my neighbor, Mrs. Applewhite, about it and—oooh wait. That's why! I only *asked* about the name. I didn't show her the envelope because she hates to be interrupted when she's on her porch kn—"

"*Knitting*. She hates to be interrupted when she's knitting. Unless, of course, you're willing to engage in idle gossip. Right?"

Phoebe felt her mouth spread into a surprised smile. "How did you know?"

He ran his hand over his hair, tousling it as he did so. "Trust me, I learned the hard way. But I *am* surprised to hear old lady Applewhite is still alive."

"Of course she's still alive. She's active and she's healthy and…" Phoebe met Tate's gaze and held it for a beat. "Anyway, as I was trying to say, I asked Mrs. Applewhite about the name on the envelope and she told me about you."

He crossed his arms against his chest. "I'll bet she did. And let me guess what she said. I turned my back on the neighborhood, right?"

Phoebe couldn't help but notice the way the man's chin jutted ever so slightly as he waited for her response, his stance bordering on rigid. It wasn't in her nature to intentionally hurt someone's feelings, but neither was lying.

"Something like that. But I'm not here to judge you or—" she motioned toward the two-story foyer visible through the open doorway "—or your lifestyle. I'm just here to deliver a letter that this other Tate Williams should have received a long time ago."

Silence fell for a moment as Phoebe shifted uncomfortably on the stone walkway and gently wrestled the letter from Kayla's pudgy little hands. It was obvious she wasn't getting anywhere with young Tate.

"Look, I'll just try a search online or something. See if I can find the right man." She turned toward her car, then stopped. "I'm sorry I wasted your time, Mr. Williams."

"It's Tate. *He* goes by Bart."

"Bart?" She turned back to the handsome man in the doorway, her mind willing her gaze to remain above the neck, to concentrate on the first real lead she'd gotten in the past ten minutes.

Tate dropped his arms to his side and nodded slowly. "Bart Williams. Tate Bartholomew Williams. He's my father."

"Your father?" The second the question left her lips she wished she could press Erase. The pain that swept across Tate Williams's face was raw and unmistakable. "I'm sorry. It's none of my business. But thank you. For the tip on his name. It might make finding him a little easier."

He looked at her strangely for a moment, his eyes searching hers. Oddly, though, the in-depth inspection didn't make her uncomfortable.

"Why don't you just let the post office deliver it? Save yourself the hassle? Especially if you've got some walls to finish and a baby to take care of."

She considered correcting his misconception but opted instead to let it slide. Really, in the grand scheme of things, what difference did it make whether she painted walls or a canvas? Probably not much to someone who lived as Tate Williams did. Someone she had no reason to ever see again.

Phoebe chose her words carefully when she answered, her tone as ambiguous as possible. "Because someone addressed this to your father nearly forty years ago. Whoever wrote this letter thought its contents were important enough to put it in an envelope and pop it in the mail. It got lost for all these years, only to turn up in *my* mailbox as your father's last known address. It's a story without an ending. Those drive me crazy."

The explanation was true enough. She *did* need life's various strings to be tied up one way or another. But the desire to deliver the misplaced letter to its rightful owner went way beyond that. To a place too personal to share with anyone—Tate Williams included.

She switched the yellowed envelope to her Kayla-holding hand and extended her empty one through the open doorway one last time, an undeniable charge surging through her body at the feel of his skin against hers when he shook it. "Thanks again, Mr. Williams. Enjoy the rest of your day."

TATE WILLIAMS WATCHED from the window as she walked to her car, his mind keenly aware of one thing. Maybe two.

Phoebe Jennings was a beautiful woman.

And he was sorry to see her go. Even if it meant visiting a part of his life he'd rather forget.

Pushing away thoughts of his father, Tate stepped slightly to the left to afford a more unobstructed view of the petite woman who'd stopped at the curb to kiss the top of her daughter's head. He couldn't help but notice the way the sunshine cast a golden glow through her soft brown hair, and the way it made his body react. Quickly and definitively.

It was hard to picture Phoebe Jennings climbing up and down ladders, painting walls for a living. Especially with such a young baby at home. But he admired her for it. Work was work. Whatever form it took.

Work.

Tate glanced down at his wristwatch and rolled his eyes. His lunch hour was virtually over and he hadn't eaten a thing. But he wasn't terribly hungry anymore, anyway. Thinking about his dad tended to have that effect.

Still, he couldn't help but wonder about the envelope a little, too. Who was it from? Who called his father Tate?

No one *he* knew.

Shrugging, he grabbed his briefcase and keys from the hall table and headed toward the garage. If he wasn't going to eat, he might as well get back to work. He peered into the kitchen as he walked by, his eyes locked on the seascape above the table. It had been a gift from his mother when he graduated from college.

"Always believe in your dreams, Tate. For when you believe in them, you will believe in yourself."

And she'd been right.

In fact, his mom had believed in him enough for the both of them. But it had never quite made up for the way his father had tried to dissuade him from his desire to be an architect. To his father, work was *building* homes. Not *designing* them.

It had been one of many points of contention between his parents in a marriage that seemed to exist solely for his benefit. While his mother had loved with her whole heart, his father had always been one step removed. As if he wanted to be somewhere else.

Shaking off the memories that threatened to ruin his day, Tate stepped into the garage toward his new red BMW convertible. Following his dreams had brought the kind of perks he could never have imagined while growing up on Quinton Lane—a place where success was measured simply by one's ability to keep food on the table. A place he'd always felt loved…until he came back from college a different person.

In their eyes, if not his own.

As he slipped his shiny new car into Reverse, he

realized he hadn't thought of the house on Quinton Lane in a very long time.

Then again, he hadn't laid eyes on Phoebe Jennings before today.

Chapter Two

Phoebe looked up from the Dolangers' canvas and reached for the gooseneck lamp to the right of her easel. The sun was slipping lower in the sky, taking with it the natural light she craved for her work. But waiting until morning to continue wasn't an option.

Not with Friday's deadline looming in just a little over sixty hours.

And not after she spent most of her day obsessing over a letter that had nothing to do with her.

She switched paintbrushes, dipping the bristles into the auburn shade she'd created to capture the exact hue of Cara Dolanger's hair. Phoebe's steady hand returned to the canvas, carefully filling in the final details of a woman who'd been difficult to immortalize.

This job had been quite a coup, the phone call coming right after a small art show of her work in downtown Cedarville. Phoebe paused for a moment as she recalled the amazing things Shane Dolanger had said when he'd hired her to paint a group portrait of his family.

"I've traveled extensively, both here and overseas. I've seen the art of some of the most renowned painters

who ever lived. Yet there is something about your work that captures the very essence of your subjects. I want you to do the same for me. And for my family."

The notion of being hired to paint a picture of the town's founding family had been thrilling. The kind of assignment that could move mountains by word of mouth alone. And when he'd told her how much he was willing to pay, she'd nearly fainted. The thought of not worrying about rent and food money for the next year was almost too hard to fathom. As was the realization that her days of working a second job to make ends meet were numbered.

It had all seemed like a dream. And in many ways it still did. But the pinch of reality was the short deadline she'd been given.

Three weeks.

Which ended in three days.

A deadline that couldn't be missed for any reason, thanks to a party the Dolangers would be throwing that same evening.

"I want our portrait to be hanging above the mantel when everyone arrives."

Phoebe had considered declining, for all of about thirty seconds. The promise of money had a way of sugar-coating reality.

Fortunately, she was a workhorse, willing to do whatever it took to complete a task. Even missing meals and getting by on very little sleep.

Unfortunately, she hadn't counted on a forty-year-old letter finding its way into her mailbox. And she certainly hadn't counted on crossing paths with Tate Williams.

Tate.

Ever since she'd left the house on Starry Night Drive, her thoughts had been returning to the man in the doorway. There was something about the man that made her suspect he could ward off life's problems with a simple hug.

And his hair? It begged to have her fingers come and play.

Shaking her head against the wave of crazy images, Phoebe forced her attention back to the canvas. There was no use dreaming about someone so different from herself. The probability of such a pairing was unlikely. And if by some fluke it *did* happen, it would never work.

Never. She'd learned that the hard way.

She glanced down at Kayla, who was happily chewing on a red block with one hand and sorting shapes with the other. Turning down Doug's offer of a lifetime supply of money in exchange for his freedom from fatherhood had hurt in ways she could never verbalize. Yet it had been freeing in a way, too. Because it was at that moment that she'd realized they didn't need him. She had not only survived childhood, but *treasured* it, thanks to her grandmother—a woman who'd loved and believed in her completely. Sure, money had been scarce, but the love in their home had more than made up for the niceties they'd been unable to buy.

If Phoebe had taken Doug's offer, she'd have been able to get Kayla anything and everything. She'd have been able to stay home and devote herself entirely to her daughter.

Turning it down had been her choice, not her lot in life as it had been for Gram. The glaring reality that resulted made Phoebe wonder, repeatedly, if she'd short-changed her daughter by choosing pride and hard work over easy living. Had she made the decision based on what was best for Kayla? A desire to show her daughter what dreams and vision could accomplish over money and entitlement? Or had it been a knee-jerk decision based on anger and pride?

It was a question Phoebe wrestled with constantly, but there it was. Because as much as she wished she could erase Doug from her mind altogether, she couldn't. He was always there, undermining her confidence and shaking her belief in herself and her talents. He was always there, flicking cash in her face as she dropped Kayla at the Haskells' so she could work— *again*. And he was there, in Kayla's rounded chin and perfectly proportioned ears, making it impossible for Phoebe to hate him completely.

How could she? If it weren't for Doug, there would be no Kayla.

And her daughter made *everything* worth it. Even a broken heart and the confidence-crushing reality that came from being stood up at the altar and offered a bribe to nev—

A loud banging from downstairs thwarted the trip down memory lane, forced Phoebe to focus on the here and now.

She dipped her brush in a cup of mineral spirits before wiping her hands on a paint-stained cloth and lifting Kayla off the floor. They made their way down the hardwood stairs and across the front hallway. The porch light had switched on in the gathering dusk, illuminating two of her neighbors on her porch.

It was hard not to groan when she saw Gertrude Applewhite and Tom Borden peeking through the glass panel that comprised the top half of Phoebe's door. Sure, she loved her neighbors, but her deadline left little time for chitchat and local gossip.

Strike that. It left *no time*. For anything.

She could say she was tired. Because she was. In a way. But the deadline-induced adrenaline coursing through her body would make that a hard sell.

She could say she had a date. But they'd insist on waiting around to check out the nonexistent guy. Anxious to see if he was good enough for their Phoebe and Kayla.

Or she could try the truth—they, of all people, would understand the importance of completing a job. Especially when paying bills and staying home with Kayla was the pot of gold at the end of the rainbow.

But even as she pulled the door open, she knew she would invite them inside. It was who she was, even to her own detriment at times. "Hi, Mrs. Applewhite, Mr. Borden. What brings you by?"

"We've got a problem, Phoebe. A big one." Tom pushed his walker through the front door, the tennis-ball-covered feet gliding easily across the hardwood floor after he'd stopped for a second to tickle Kayla's cheek.

Fear gripped Phoebe's stomach as she looked from Mrs. Applewhite's ashen skin to Mr. Borden's troubled eyes. "What's wrong? Did Ms. Weatherby pass?"

Eunice Weatherby lived two doors down. A spitfire mentally, the century-old woman suffered from a host of physical ailments.

Mrs. Applewhite waved her hands in the air as she rounded the corner into Phoebe's sitting room, visibly irritated by the fact that Mr. Borden had reached the room first. "Eunice is fine. Ornery as ever, but fine."

Phoebe took a slow calming breath then perched on the sofa beside Mr. Borden as Kayla pulled on her hair and squealed. "Then what's wrong?"

"It's them council folks. They want to take over our neighborhood green space," Mr. Borden explained as he ran a hand across his coarse, gray hair.

"Can I have some water, Phoebe? I'm parched."

Phoebe flashed a grin at Mr. Borden as he rolled his eyes. "Of course, Mrs. Applewhite. Mr. Borden? Would you like some, too?"

"Yes, he'll take some. He needs more water. Helps with regularity."

"I'll speak for myself, Gertrude." Mr. Borden turned wary eyes in Phoebe's direction and nodded, a slight smile tugging at his lined mouth. "That would be nice, Phoebe, thank you."

She set the baby on the floor near the sofa and disappeared into the kitchen. As she pulled two glasses from the cabinet beside the sink she couldn't help but smile at the sound of Kayla happily babbling away with their unexpected company—a common occurrence that was as good for Kayla as it was for their neighbors. Nothing could bring Phoebe's grandmother back, but raising Kayla in this environment was the next best thing.

When she returned with ice-filled water glasses, Phoebe glanced at the clock on the mantel. Eight minutes gone already.

"So tell me about this council thing. They want to take over *our* green space?"

Mr. Borden nodded. Mrs. Applewhite grunted.

"Sure as shootin' they do. And *why?* Because they say

we don't take care of it. Like those daffodils I plant every year aren't good enough. What more do they want?"

Phoebe waited patiently for Mrs. Applewhite's diatribe to end. "What *do* they want?" she finally asked, her eyes focused on Mr. Borden's face.

"Something different. Something unique. It's part of this Clean Up Cedarville campaign they're all jabbering about." Tom raised a shaking glass to his lips and took a long, slow sip before continuing. "But to clean our space up the way they want it cleaned up—to make it different and unique—costs money. Money we ain't had for a long time."

"What happens if we don't?"

Mrs. Applewhite crossed her bony arms across her stomach and huffed. "If we don't, the city takes it over."

Phoebe was missing something. She had to be.

"And why is that bad? They'd be making it unique on *their* dime."

Mr. Borden set his glass down on the coffee table and fingered the top bar of his walker. "That space has belonged to this neighborhood since I was Kayla's age. I know that doesn't mean much to folks these days, but it means something to me." The elderly man's voice deepened, his eyes narrowing as if he was picturing things she could only visit through his words. "I'm not dumb, Phoebe. I know it's nothing more than an empty lot with pretty flowers. I know it doesn't have all the trappings of a real park. But it comes to life just fine whenever we need it. Always has."

Suddenly it made sense. It was about tradition. A well-earned, time-honored tradition that was being threatened by people who simply didn't understand.

She reached out and touched his cold, leathery hand. "We'll figure this out. We'll find a way to make that space unique. A way to keep it for the neighborhood as it was intended."

Mr. Borden nodded, a hint of moisture in his eyes. "I don't know how any of us can come up with that kind of money. We're all on a fixed income. And you're barely making ends meet yourself, Phoebe."

"We'll figure it out. If I get this portrait done in time, I'll be working a big shindig Friday night. I agreed to this particular party because the pay is more than usual *and* I'll get to be the proverbial fly on the wall as guests see my work. We can use *that* money."

"The kind of 'unique' these people want is going to require more than *one* job," Mrs. Applewhite said sadly.

Mr. Borden stood and motioned for her to do likewise. "We've taken enough of Phoebe's time for this evening. Let's go, Gertrude." To Phoebe he said, "Your offer is very kind. Thank you."

"Perhaps a few bake sales…" Mrs. Applewhite murmured.

Phoebe trailed behind her neighbors as they made their way to her front hallway, the elderly woman's comment taking hold in her mind. "That could work. A little here and a little there could add up to a lot. Let me get through Friday and we can talk again over the weekend, have a neighborhood meeting. I'm sure Eunice will have some ideas. Mr. and Mrs. Haskell, too."

They were almost at the door when Mrs. Applewhite turned, her eyes magnified to twice their size behind her thick glasses. "So, did you speak to him?"

"Him?" Phoebe tried to follow the change in conversation but her thoughts were still sifting through money-making schemes even as her gaze tracked a crawling baby in desperate search of a furry tail to pull.

"The uppity one."

The uppity one?

"Oh! You mean, Tate Williams?"

"Who else?" Mrs. Applewhite snapped.

Phoebe walked around the pair and pulled the door open. "Yes. I did."

"Rude, I bet."

"I'm not sure I'd say rude, exactly. A little caught off guard, perhaps."

"I'd say rude." Mrs. Applewhite nearly shoved Mr. Borden through the door in her usual brusque manner. "Rude is rude. And that young man is rude."

"It doesn't matter much. The person I was *really* looking for wasn't there." Phoebe stepped onto the porch and inhaled deeply, enjoying the refreshing night air.

"You're talking gibberish, Phoebe. You just said you spoke to him. And you *did* ask me about Tate Williams, right?"

Phoebe pulled out her scrunchie and let her hair tumble down her back. "It was just a miscommunication, that's all. It was his *dad* I was looking for."

"Bart? Well, why didn't you say so?" Mrs. Applewhite jutted her chin forward and eyed Phoebe curiously. "I could have spared you the displeasure of meeting Mr. Rude and sent you where you needed to go."

Phoebe stared at her neighbor. "You know how I can find Tate's dad?"

"Of course. Once a Quinton Laner, always a Quinton Laner. Unless you're Tate Williams. Then you're nothing."

TATE WILLIAMS LOOKED UP from his plans as Regina Melvey strode into his office, coffeepot in hand. In the five years he'd been with McDonald and Murphy, he'd never had a more efficient—intuitive—secretary than Regina.

"Coffee, Mr. Williams?"

Pushing back in his desk chair, he nodded, his cheeks briefly inflating with a frustrated exhalation. "Sounds great. I could use an artificial boost right about now."

"Still monkeying around with that new Dolanger office building?" Regina leaned over the desk and refilled his empty mug from the steaming pot. "It's looked wonderful each of the last five times you've shown it to me."

Tate grinned at the fiftysomething woman, taking in the way her gray hair curled softly around her face in much the same way his mom's had. "Point noted. But there's something about the entrance area that's just not clicking."

He motioned her over to the drafting table. "See? Right here." He pointed at the area surrounding the main doorway. "It's not jelling with the rest of the building."

Silence settled over the room as his secretary leaned over the sketch of the Dolanger Enterprises building and ran her fingers across the trouble spot. Finally, she spoke. "It feels closed up."

Closed up.

"That's it!" Tate reached up from his seat and cupped her face, pulling her toward him for a great big kiss on her forehead. "Regina, you are a genius."

"Moi?" she asked with mock surprise, one carefully manicured hand resting at her throat.

Tate laughed. *"Vous."*

"Good. I'm glad. Now if it's okay, I'm going to head out for the night. The dogs are probably tearing up the house."

He checked his watch. "Oh, Regina. I'm sorry. Why are you still here? You should have left hours ago."

She hoisted the coffeepot into the air. "You work late, I work late. We're a team, remember?"

How could he forget? Since the day she'd reported in as his secretary, Regina Melvey had become irreplaceable. In less than a week she'd managed to learn his subtle cues on everything from when quiet was preferred to those times when he needed a sounding board. In a matter of months she'd managed to become not only his righthand person at work, but also his friend. She knew about the various dates he'd gone on over the past few years, listened to the countless reasons why there was never a second. She'd been there with a box of tissues and an understanding shoulder when his mom passed away, and a listening ear when he'd hit his limit with his dad.

He reached out and squeezed her hand gently. "If I get this partnership, you'll get a raise."

"Raise, schmaise. If you get this partnership, you can buy me some flowers and a chocolate cake."

"You're on." He grinned as he watched her walk toward his office door, his mood brighter now that he knew how his sketch needed to be fixed.

"Oh, and you can help me paint my porch," she called over her shoulder as she stepped into the hall.

Paint.

It really shouldn't have surprised him how fast that one word pulled his thoughts back to his lunchtime visitor. Not when he factored in how much he'd thought of her already that day.

Her long, soft brown hair. Her khaki-green eyes. Her hesitant smile. Her beautiful lips. Her persistence.

"Regina?"

The woman stuck her head back in the doorway. "Yes, boss?"

"Can I ask you something?"

"Of course."

Tate ran a hand across his face and through his hair as he counted to ten under his breath. "You were close to your parents. Did you know much about their single years? You know, before they married and had you?"

He felt her studying him as she seemed to weigh her answer. When she finally spoke, her voice was soft yet clear. "A little. But my parents were grade school sweethearts. They really didn't have a life without each other."

"I see."

"Why do you ask?"

"Something happened today that made me wonder about my dad's life before me. Before my mother. But it's no big deal, I guess. Just a fleeting question."

The woman fingered the silver pendant hanging from a chain around her neck and hesitated briefly. "You could ask him, you know."

"No. I can't." Tate was anxious to put an end to a conversation he never should have started. "Hey, have fun with the dogs tonight."

"I will. But—" Regina gripped the coffeepot with both hands and shifted from foot to foot "—there's something different about you since you came back from lunch."

"Different? How so?" he asked.

"Well, I've heard you whistling a few times. Did something happen?"

In addition to being the world's best secretary, Regina was also amazingly perceptive when it came to people. So perceptive, in fact, she often sensed his mood before he did.

He shrugged. "The only thing that happened over lunch—besides me not eating—was an unexpected delivery. Only it wasn't for me. I felt kind of bad for her, though, because she seemed genuinely disappointed when I told her I wasn't the right person."

"She?"

"Yeah. She."

"Hmm." The woman looked at him one more time, the curiosity in her eyes as tangible as the knowing smile on her face. "Was she pretty?"

Uh-oh. He knew where this was going.

"Yes."

"Friendly?"

"Hard to tell. But I'd say *genuine.*"

"Hmm," Regina repeated.

"What's that supposed to mean?"

"The whistling makes sense now."

He held up his hands, palms outward. "Whoa. Slow down there, Regina. I probably just had a song stuck in my head from the car. Besides, she had a baby with her. A little girl."

Regina's left eyebrow cocked upward. "Did she have a ring?"

He shook his head. He'd noticed the absence of a wedding band immediately. And he hadn't missed the way she'd corrected him on his use of the word *Mrs*.

"Maybe she was babysitting," Regina offered.

"No, it was hers."

"Okay. Maybe it was. Either way—" the secretary's lips twitched— "you were *whistling*, boss."

Tate dropped his head into his hands.

Regina laughed softly. "I won't ask you anything more until that sketch is done. But when it is…"

He peeked out from behind his hands. "Skedaddle, Regina."

"Yes, boss." She stepped back into the hall, then stopped. "Oh, I called Shane Dolanger as you requested and confirmed your attendance at his party on Friday. His secretary said he'd be delighted."

"Thanks. I'll be delighted, too—if I finish his plans." Tate looked back at the sketch on his drafting table, already envisioning the changes he needed to make. Regina was right. It was the closed-up feeling that had been eating at him all afternoon. A wider appearance to the entranceway would create a more welcoming look. Draw people in. An essential component of any successful business.

But even as he bent over the table for the umpteenth time that day, his sense of design was being overshadowed by one persistent thought.

Regina was right. He had a ringless Phoebe Jennings on the brain.

Chapter Three

Phoebe couldn't help but feel a sense of pride as she walked into her art room and noticed the jars of paint neatly organized on the shelf above her worktable. The assortment of colors, lined up like a row of infantry soldiers, was proof positive she'd really finished the portrait.

She'd dropped it by Shane Dolanger's office earlier in the day, but somehow its completion had seemed almost surreal—a familiar symptom of the postproject fog that rolled into her brain the second she finished an assignment.

Phoebe grabbed her silver link watch from around the gooseneck lamp and fastened it to her wrist. Although a huge part of her wished she could retrieve Kayla from the Haskells' and cuddle with her all night, there was another part—the one dubbed Probing Phoebe by her grandmother—that couldn't wait to get to the Dolanger party. And it had nothing whatsoever to do with carrying trays of hors d'oeuvres through rooms the size of her whole house.

Quite the contrary, in fact.

It was about people's reactions. *Wealthy* people's reactions.

To *her* art.

She'd been raised by her grandmother to know people from opposite sides of the train tracks didn't mix, that the discrepancies in upbringing and life experiences made it impossible to connect in any meaningful way. Phoebe had thought the notion was ludicrous until she'd ignored her grandmother's warning and dated across the divide shortly after graduating from college. The result had been disastrous. With Kayla the biggest victim of all.

But this was different. This wasn't about human relationships. This was about ability and talent, hard work and perseverance. None of which were dictated by money.

A gentle push on her ankle made her look down and smile.

"Hey there, Boots." Phoebe squatted down and ran a gentle hand across the calico tabby's back. "I can't pick you up, old guy, or I'll get all furry. And we can't have that at a West Cedarville party, can we?"

The soulful yellow eyes blinked back at her.

"Now I know what you're thinking. You were Gram's cat for far too long not to have been influenced by her notions. And you're both right. It's time to quit the serving job—I know that. But I couldn't quit until *after* I'd finished the portrait, and I wouldn't have felt right bailing without giving any notice. Besides, tonight was just too good to pass up. I mean, think about it…I'll get to see my portrait on the wall of Shane Dolanger's home. See how people react to it." Phoebe stood, picking a few orange-and-white strands of hair from her sleeve.

As much as she'd love to be the kind of person who didn't need validation from others, she wasn't. Artists rarely were. Accolades were food for the creative soul.

Still, she knew it went beyond that this time. The Dolangers' party had unparalleled potential to take that validation and translate it into paying jobs. Lots of them.

That news of her success could eventually wind its way back to Doug's family was simply the cherry on top.

The *chocolate-dipped* cherry.

Surrounded by the fluffiest whipped cream ever.

Pulling the last of Boots's hair from her clothes, Phoebe glanced around her studio one last time, let her eyes rest on the picture of Kayla near the upper left corner of her worktable. Kayla with her chubby cheeks, cherubic mouth and beautiful smile...

Kayla.

Phoebe hated spending another night away from her daughter, hated having to leave her at the Haskells' yet again—their home alive with Kayla's happy babbling while Phoebe's was eerily quiet. But if there was any consolation at all, it was knowing tonight would be the last time. The paycheck from the Dolangers' portrait would enable her to finally concentrate on her art—something she could do with Kayla by her side.

A picture of Phoebe's grandmother sat in a frame beside Kayla's, and as she glanced at it, a familiar pang of hurt made it difficult to breathe. "I did it, Gram. I really and truly did it."

It was a day her grandmother had always believed would come. A day she'd first predicted when Phoebe had been barely ten years old.

"You keep on painting, sweetheart. And you never give up. It's how dreams come true."

Indeed.

Kissing her fingertips softly, Phoebe brought them to

the woman's face, let them linger for the briefest of moments. "Thanks for believing in me, Gram."

With a flick of the overhead light switch, she made her way down the aging wooden staircase to the main floor, willing her heart to look forward. Gram was gone. There wasn't anything Phoebe could do to change that. But she could enjoy her moment in the spotlight for both of them—even if it was from the shadows, with a serving tray in her hand.

Stopping beside the antique table in the foyer, Phoebe fastened first the buttons at her left wrist and then the buttons at her right. The crisp white fabric of the blouse hugged her body well, as did the black dress pants the caterer required. A quick glance in the mirror above the table revealed a face that was a bit paler than she'd like, though that was understandable after spending nearly every waking hour of the past three weeks holed up in her art room. Except, of course, when she'd trekked out to Tate Williams's house.

Tate.

As infuriating as the man had been, she couldn't get him off her mind. Was she so desperate for male companionship she'd be lured by a handsome face and gorgeous body? Hadn't she learned a thing from the experience with Doug?

She pulled her purse onto the table and began rummaging for some blush. Though thoughts of Tate had just brought ample color to her cheeks, she noted.

"Ugh. I've got Tate Williams on the brain," Phoebe groaned as she dropped the colored powder back into her bag and reached, instead, for some mascara. As she unscrewed the cap, her gaze drifted from the mirror to the table, settled on the envelope she'd been trying desperately to ignore.

It was just as she'd told the man's son. Stories without endings drove her nuts. Always had. It was *the* single reason her grandmother had moved up bedtime preparations by a full thirty minutes when Phoebe was little. Books could not be closed midway. Not when *she* was listening.

But her mission to deliver the letter to Tate's father wasn't just about endings and closure. It was also about regret. The kind of nagging regret she lived with on a daily basis, thanks to the many opportunities she'd missed, chances to tell her grandmother just how much she loved her before it was too late. At least whoever had sent the letter had *tried* to communicate.

The chime of Gram's grandfather clock at the end of the hallway snapped her attention back to the task at hand. "Okay, Boots, I'm leaving," she called up the steps as she pulled her keys from her purse and strode toward the front door.

She'd been pleased at how quickly the three of them had warmed to their new place. This town had been a welcome change from living with the memories locked in Gram's old house. And little by little, it was beginning to feel like home. Partly because it was an older house, like Gram's, and partly because the elderly neighbors she'd grown to love over the past six months provided a link of sorts to a woman she'd loved from the day she was born.

She followed the side path to the driveway and hopped into the small blue Fiesta she'd purchased with what was left of Gram's estate after paying the last of the medical bills. The engine purred to life and she backed slowly onto the street, watching for any of the assortment of neighbors that lingered on the sidewalks prior to the dinner hour each evening.

The drive to West Cedarville was slow going, with businesspeople heading home from work in anticipation of the weekend. It wasn't hard to pick out who was heading where regardless of what direction they were driving. The cars themselves told the story. The smaller sedans and pickup trucks headed east. The expensive SUVs and luxury cars headed west. And in that instant Phoebe knew what it meant to swim upstream. Fiestas didn't belong at this end of town. Not unless they were being driven by the maid. Or the gardener.

Or maybe even the painter.

She laughed to herself as she pulled into the Dolangers's gated driveway and stopped at the intercom.

"Yes?" The voice that emerged from the small, wall-mounted black box was crisp and efficient, if just a little bored.

"Phoebe Jennings."

"Phoebe Jennings…" The voice trailed off, a pretty good indication the person was checking a list of some sort.

"I'm one of the servers."

"One moment, let me check *that* list. Yes, here you are. I'll buzz you through. Park off to the side and come through the back door. Do not access the circular drive in front."

She nodded automatically then maneuvered her car through the now-open wrought-iron gate. The side driveway wasn't hard to locate; it was where the other

Fiesta-like cars were parked. One for the maid, one for the gardener, one for the portrait spy.

Once inside it didn't take long for her to learn her duties, as well as the dos and don'ts of the evening—a list that stopped just shy of "don't steal the silverware." Not that it mattered. She couldn't care less about the silverware or the china or any of the priceless knickknacks strewn throughout the palatial home.

The only thing she cared about was in the hearth room.

No matter how many of these parties he attended on behalf of the firm, Tate never felt entirely comfortable. In fact, if he thought about it, he felt more like a run-of-the-mill goldfish in a Japanese koi pond.

But it wasn't the expensive cars lined up in the driveway that made him feel out of place—his sporty red Beemer held its own quite nicely. And it wasn't the designer clothes his fellow guests would invariably be wearing—he had more than his fair share of Zenga shirts and slacks.

It was the stuff you *couldn't* see that turned him off. The aloofness that came and went depending on who was around. The unwritten sport of one-upmanship between close friends. The look-but-don't-touch aura that clung to so many like overbearing cologne. The puffed out chests of the über-rich.

He preferred the kind of people he'd grown up with—quiet, unassuming, hardworking types.

"The kind who turned their back on you, buddy," he mumbled to himself as he rang the bell to the left of the Dolangers's massive oak front door.

A dignified-looking man of about sixty pulled the door open and welcomed him inside. "Your name, sir?"

"Tate. Tate Williams."

"I will let Mr. and Mrs. Dolanger know you have arrived, Mr. Williams. Please make yourself comfortable."

He followed the man's gesture and started down a long hallway, noticing the unusual lines and details of the home. Although the money was in designing state-of-the-art office buildings for corporations, his heart was in smaller projects where creativity and experimentation had freer reign.

A burst of laughter from a room off the left side of the hallway made him stop. He poked his head through the doorway and looked around at the sea of unfamiliar faces, at the guests engaged in conversations in every professionally decorated corner of the large living area.

He kept walking.

If Regina were here, she'd tell him he was in a foul mood. That it was time to shake off whatever was bothering him and get on with things. And she'd be right, as always.

Problem was, he wasn't quite sure where the mood had come from.

He'd finished the plans for Dolanger's building and presented them to the CEO and his board earlier that day. Their enthusiasm and immediate approval had been the validation he'd expected. The sketch was dynamite and he knew it. Having his boss there to witness the accolades had been the cherry on top in terms of furthering his likelihood of being named a partner in the firm.

So really, Tate had no reason to be anything but all smiles.

Yet he wasn't.

Because the moment he'd stepped out of Dolanger's

board meeting, the one thought he'd been avoiding all week resurfaced with a vengeance.

His dad.

Ever since Phoebe Jennings had appeared on his doorstep with the letter, his mind had been toying with the question of who'd sent it. And why.

No one called his father Tate. Not even his mom.

Tate rounded the final corner of the hallway and stopped.

Somehow, in the middle of what felt more like a museum than a house, was the most welcoming room he'd ever seen on this side of Cedarville. The walls were of wood paneling with stone trim, the ceiling traversed by thick wooden beams that stretched from one end to the other. Wrought-iron chains hung sporadically from the space between the beams, each strand holding an old-fashioned lantern. Three picture windows had cushioned window seats—the kind you could lose yourself in for hours with a good book. Large mahogany bookcases were scattered throughout the room, each one boasting as many framed pictures and special family heirlooms as they did actual novels and story collections.

It was the kind of room his mom would have loved.

Tate wandered across the quiet room to the fireplace, a large stone affair with a mahogany mantel that ran the entire length of the wall. But it wasn't the unusual stone that was used or the thickness of the mantel wood that held his attention. It was the portrait that hung above it, a warm, loving, beautifully painted likeness of Shane and Cara Dolanger with their three children.

Suddenly, the people who lived in this home seemed real. The kind of people who sat on a couch and watched television as a family, vacationed at amusement parks and spent hours hunched over a Monopoly board together. The antithesis of what he'd imagined as he'd viewed the rest of the house.

The sound of soft footsteps made him turn, his eyes widening as he took in the woman standing quietly behind him. Her slender yet curvy body was smartly clad in black slacks and a white dress shirt, and she was holding a serving platter.

"Miss Jennings?" The disbelief in his voice mirrored the look in her eyes as she pulled her attention from above his head and fixed it on his face.

"Oh. Wow. Mr. Williams. I'm— I didn't know any-one was… I didn't know you were in here. I'm sorry." She turned to go.

"Wait. Don't leave on my account." Without think-ing, he reached out and touched her arm, turning her gently. "I didn't know you'd be here."

She held the tray in his direction. "Would you like some caviar?"

Tate reluctantly pulled his hand away and waved it in the air. "Nah. Hate the stuff. I'm more of a meatball, mini hot dog kind of guy."

He was rewarded with a shy smile.

"I haven't seen any meatballs or mini hot dogs, but I'll keep an eye out for you." Phoebe looked around quickly. "Technically, I'm not supposed to be in here. I'm assigned to the back patio, not the house. But I just had to see how it looked…"

He watched as her eyes left his face and traveled over his head once again.

"Um, don't mind me. I better get back to my post,"

she said, the inflection in her voice conveying a note of disappointment.

"Wait! Don't go." Tate glanced over his shoulder quickly, realized she was looking at the same portrait that had drawn him across the room. "You came to see *this,* didn't you? It's phenomenal."

The woman's high cheekbones reddened noticeably as she shifted the tray from one hand to the other. "You really think so?" she asked quietly.

"How could I not? It caught my eye from over there—" he pointed to the arched entrance that led to the hallway "—and that's pretty amazing for a guy who'd normally be drawn to the architecture of this room."

"Thank you."

Confused, he bobbed his head to the left to recapture her attention. "Thank you? For what?"

She tried, unsuccessfully, to tuck a strand of hair into her bun as she seemed to contemplate his question. But just as she was starting to reply, a noisy group of four burst in through a different archway, chatting up a storm.

"I better get back to work."

"Wait!" Tate knew he sounded like a desperate idiot, but he didn't really care. He had questions to ask. "What are you doing here? I thought you were a *painter.*"

For a few moments Phoebe was busy offering hors d'oeuvres to the guests. But when they moved on across the room, her gaze focused once again on him.

"I am—by day. This—" she nodded at the tray in her hand "—is my second job."

"You work two jobs *and* take care of a baby?"

A flash of something that resembled pain crossed her

face. "You do what you have to do, Mr. Williams. Kayla knows I love her."

A moment of silence fell as his words came back to haunt him. "Wait. I didn't mean that the way it sound—"

She held up her free hand. "I need to get back to work."

Desperate to undo his rudeness and keep their connection, he said the first thing that popped into his head. "Hey. I know a friend who needs his rec room painted. I'd be happy to put in a good word for you."

"I don't paint walls, Mr. Williams. I paint port—ohh, it doesn't matter." Her words were crisp and matter-of-fact as they emerged through lips that were no longer smiling.

"But your clothes. Your car. I thought—"

"You *assumed,* Mr. Williams. There's a difference."

He felt his mouth drop open as Phoebe Jennings turned on her heel and walked briskly from the room. And in that instant, he felt an awful lot like the supercilious party-goers he'd been mentally slamming when he arrived.

"Good going, Tate. Good going," he mumbled under his breath.

"Shane was right. That portrait *is* amazing!"

His cheeks warm, Tate looked from the foursome on his right to the framed canvas above the fireplace, Phoebe's words echoing in his brain.

"I don't paint walls, Mr. Williams."

Suddenly it made perfect sense why she'd left her post to see the family portrait. Why her voice had grown quiet, yet strangely hopeful, as he'd praised the artwork hanging above the mantel.

He was an idiot. A self-righteous idiot.

Chapter Four

The flow of money-making ideas had slowed to a crawl over the past hour, though not from a lack of trying. There were simply some suggestions that just wouldn't work. Not with the Quinton Lane demographic, anyway.

"I still think a dog wash could make a small fortune. There's a lot of lazy people out there."

Phoebe forced her gaze to remain on her next-door neighbor's face despite the urge to roll her eyes. Bake sales and knitting classes were one thing, but soapsuds and old people didn't mix.

"I think—" Phoebe nibbled her lower lip briefly, determined to squash further discussion of a dog wash once and for all. "I'm just afraid that if we did that, the soapy runoff would ruin the flower beds you worked so hard to plant, Mrs. Applewhite. And then we'd have to spend even more money recreating your hard work."

"Excellent point there, Phoebe." Tom Borden shifted in his seat and cast a sly wink in her direction.

"Flowers, schmowers," Eunice Weatherby, declared. "With the way all of you shuffle around like wounded penguins, washing a dog would land someone in the hospital with a metal bolt in their hip, and the city would ding us for violating some unknown old people code."

Phoebe smacked her hand over her mouth in an attempt to stifle the laugh that threatened to earn her an evil eye or two. But she was too late.

"Don't you glare at Phoebe, Gertrude. You know I'm right." Eunice pulled the flaps of her thin cotton sweater closer to her frail body and leaned back in the white wooden rocker. "Eighty-year-olds have no business washing dogs. We need something practical. Intelligent."

Leave it to the lone centurion to call a spade a spade.

A sea of cotton-tops nodded in unison.

"Eunice is dead-on. Though I must point out that I'm younger than the rest of you, you know." Tom Borden's face lit up with a mischievous grin, a comforting change to an expression that had looked so troubled only an hour ago. "We've got some good ideas but I still think we can come up with something better."

Again, heads nodded.

"How about a Quinton Lane tag sale?" Phoebe suggested, as she looked from one spectacled face to the other.

"You mean like a garage sale?" Martha Haskell leaned over and smoothed Kayla's hair back as the baby stopped, midcrawl, to check out an ant.

Phoebe gently clapped her hands together and smiled as Kayla left the insect in favor of a cuddle. Once her daughter was situated on her lap, busy with a sippy cup of juice, she turned her attention to the woman who cared for Kayla whenever Phoebe had to work.

"It's exactly like a garage sale. Only instead of having people walk from garage to garage, we could set our things on tables along the sidewalk." Phoebe kissed the pudgy little hand that reached up to her mouth. "It would be a way to get rid of things we don't need while earning some nice money for our project."

"Finally, we have something." Eunice's voice, shaky and low, cut through the various conversations that followed Phoebe's explanation. "And it doesn't involve slipping and sliding and the *whoop-whoop* of an ambulance. Though, the paramedics tend to be lookers, don't they? Almost makes the bills worth it."

Phoebe quietly kissed the top of the baby's head as laughter erupted around them. The youngest by almost fifty years, she never felt out of place with this crowd. They'd welcomed her and Kayla into the neighborhood with open arms, making them feel as if they, too, were natives of Quinton Lane.

"I hate to break things up," Gertrude Applewhite said, peering over her silver-rimmed glasses at everyone. "But what are we going to *do* with the money?"

The laughter ceased and all eyes turned to Phoebe.

Uh-oh. She hadn't come up with actual plans for the green space project yet. The amount of money they raised would dictate the possibilities.

Fortunately, Tom Borden voiced that very sentiment, encouraging everyone to take one thing at a time. And to stay positive. "Why don't we all think of some ideas over the next few days and meet again next weekend, after we see how the tag sales does? In the meantime, I'll call my friend at the paper and get word out on our sale. Think we can get it together for next Saturday? We don't have a lot of time to play with if we're going to get the city off our backs."

By the time the meeting was officially over, Kayla

had drifted to sleep in Phoebe's arms, her sippy cup resting lightly against her bottom lip.

"She's a real beauty, just like her mom." Mr. Borden wrapped his hands around the sides of his walker and glided along beside them as they headed toward the two small steps that led to Gertrude Applewhite's front walk.

"Thanks, Mr. Borden." Phoebe held Kayla's head to her shoulder as she leaned over and brushed a soft kiss on the elderly man's pale cheek. Her own grandfather had died long before she was born, and her relationship with her grandmother had been so special she'd never really stopped to think what it would have been like to have one. But if she had, she was fairly confident she'd have envisioned someone just like Tom Borden. Quiet and introspective, gentle and compassionate, patient and thoughtful.

Phoebe waved goodbye to the rest of her neighbors then gently shifted Kayla in her arms as she turned toward home. She hadn't gone two steps when she heard her name being called. Turning around, she groaned inwardly.

Mrs. Applewhite.

"Did you give Bart his letter yet?" The woman rested her wrinkled hands on her hips, revealing the plump waist that had been hidden under her brightly colored polyester housecoat throughout the morning.

"No. Not yet. But that's where we're headed once naptime is over."

And it was true. They were. It just so happened Phoebe had already made a half dozen mental visits to the man over the past few hours. She'd envisioned the retirement community where Bart Williams lived, imagined his reaction when she handed him the letter, guessed at its contents again and again—

"At least you don't have to deal with his insufferable son any longer." Mrs. Applewhite twisted on her heels and marched back up the porch steps.

"If only it was that simple," Phoebe mumbled to herself.

Her neighbor was right. She didn't have to see Tate Williams ever again. She had Bart's address and she wouldn't be serving at the kind of parties Tate attended any longer.

But that was just it—it wasn't about what she *had* to do, it was about what she *wanted* to do. And therein lay the problem.

Sure, he'd been annoying when she'd first met him, but only because he was trying to be friendly and playful rather than compliant and forthcoming as she'd wanted.

At the Dolangers' house she'd even snapped at him. He hadn't condemned her heavy work schedule, just expressed surprise. It was her own insecurity that had sparked the unfair leap. Tate Williams had no way of knowing her biggest fear in life was about not finding the correct balance between her dreams and her daughter. He wasn't privy to the daily mental hammering Phoebe gave herself on that subject.

And as for his offer to recommend her for a job, it was a thoughtful gesture, with no hidden maliciousness. He'd had no reason to think she was an artist. *She* was the one who'd refused to correct his wall-painting theory the first day they'd met.

She owed the man an apology. A big one. And that alone was a good enough reason for thinking about him all morning. But she knew it was more than that. Much more.

The desire to apologize couldn't explain the way she'd mentally ogled him over and over while her neighbors brainstormed ways to save their green space.

Lust and attraction explained that.

TATE DROVE SLOWLY past each house, an undeniable mixture of peace and tension threading through his body. It was both comforting and unsettling to realize nothing had changed in the four years he'd been avoiding the place.

In fact, aside from fairly massive tree growth, a few new roofs and a smattering of freshly painted porch railings, not much had changed since he'd been a little boy growing up on Quinton Lane.

Some of his fondest childhood memories came from times spent in these homes, with the families who lived inside. Hide-and-seek in Johnny Haskell's backyard, homemade lemonade on Ms. Weatherby's front porch, designing birdhouses with Mr. Borden, ducking for cover from Mrs. Applewhite….

It was the kind of past that seemed almost idyllic in nature. The kind of life experiences that formed a man. A good, solid, hardworking man.

Yet somehow the neighbors hadn't seen it that way.

He felt his stomach tense as he neared his childhood home, a place that could be either warm and cozy or cold and distant, depending on something as simple as whether his mother had been home or not. It was a truth he still wrestled with even now that she was gone, any common ground with his father having died along with her.

Suddenly Tate regretted his decision to come back. The past was just that—the past. He'd moved on. And there was no sense in looking back. He deserved better.

Unfortunately, so did Phoebe Jennings. Which meant he had to tolerate a few memories whether he liked it or not.

Shifting down, Tate slowly coasted to a stop across the street from Phoebe's front door. The mere thought of the beautiful woman who lived inside had a way of making his core temperature rise and his mind wander to thoughts of kissing her exquisite lips and wrapping his arms around her tiny waist.

Crazy, he knew. But an indisputable fact regardless of the sudden tightness in his pants.

Great.

If he didn't knock it off he wouldn't be able to get out of the car, let alone talk to the woman. An option he refused to accept. Instead, he forced himself to focus on something other than Phoebe Jennings while his lust-ometer settled down. Fortunately, the small crowd of individuals slowly dispersing from Gertrude Applewhite's front porch was a great place to start.

He knew these people. Knew their families and where they lived. Knew their triumphs and hardships. Knew their likes and dislikes.

Sure, they'd aged. The walkers and hunched postures were evidence of that. But their expressions, their auras, were the same. Mr. Borden pushed his walker across the porch with the same lighthearted step he'd possessed back when Tate was a little boy. Ms. Weatherby looked heartbroken at the assistance she needed to get down the steps, yet recovered her pride and dignity the second her feet hit the concrete. Mrs. Haskell still looked as if she'd pop around the corner with a plate of homemade cookies, despite the thick glasses and snow-white hair that hadn't been there when he and Johnny were friends. Tate's thoughts traveled back in time as he watched his best friend's mom wave goodbye to an attractive woman holding a baby—

Phoebe.

He sat, motionless, as he watched her turn to talk to Mrs. Applewhite, a sleeping Kayla cuddled in her arms. Despite her age—which he gauged to be midtwenties—Phoebe Jennings looked completely at home with her elderly neighbors. Her smile was genuine, her posture carefree. He felt a yearning in his body as she tightened her arms around the baby with an air of innocence and vulnerability—qualities he'd missed the first two times they'd met.

Though, technically, *missed* was probably the wrong word. His bizarre knack for sticking his foot in his mouth whenever they were together probably chased away those traits in favor of disbelief and dislike. Maybe even revulsion.

But today would be different. He'd make sure of that. He wanted her to see him for who he was, not the insensitive Neanderthal he'd been at the Dolangers' party.

Ever since she'd walked out of the hearth room last night, he hadn't been able to get her out of his mind. Guilt, perhaps. At least partly. But it was more than that. Because he knew darn well his thinking about her had begun the day she'd showed up at his home, letter in hand.

He'd pictured her often in the days since, imagined what it would be like to kiss her. To hold her. To have her.

And it wasn't hard to know why.

Phoebe Jennings was a beautiful woman. Anyone could see that. But it was the other stuff that made him dream about her—the shy smile, the genuine heart, the hardworking soul. She was a woman who, by all appearances, was a good mother. Something he respected more than anything else.

Propelled by the idea of seeing her again, Tate stepped from his car and crossed the quiet street, his slick red sports car standing out like a sore thumb among vehicles that were decades old. His pace quickened to a trot as Phoebe turned up her walkway.

"Hey, Phoebe! Hold up a sec."

She turned and looked at him, the corners of her mouth turning upward in what appeared to be a smile. Wishful thinking, perhaps. But he'd take it.

"Well, look who's here."

A shrill voice he remembered from his youth drew his attention to the right, to the sight of Gertrude Applewhite's pursed lips and narrowed eyes.

Oh, boy.

It was amazing how a simple tone and expression could transport a person back in time. For Tate, at that moment, it was as if he was standing once again, beside Johnny Haskell on the sidewalk, their hair sweaty from kickball, their shoelaces untied. And there in front of them was Mrs. Applewhite, chewing them out for some life-shattering offense such as spitting too close to her driveway or leaving a footprint in her mulch.

"Hi there, Mrs. Applewhite. You look nice today." He

stopped as he reached the sidewalk and waved his hand in the elderly woman's direction.

"Save the pleasantries, Tate. I see right through them. Why don't you turn around, get back in that flashy status symbol of yours and go back where you came from?"

He felt his fists tighten at his sides, his shoulders tense. For years he'd held his tongue, conducted himself according to his mother's teachings of respecting one's elders. But he'd had enough. Even his mother would have wanted him to stand up for what was right—although *her* words would have been far more diplomatic than the ones running through his head at that moment.

Still, it was long overdue.

He opened his mouth to speak, to tell the woman exactly what he thought of her, when he felt a hand grip his arm. A touch so gentle and so warm that his skin tingled in response.

And as he looked down into Phoebe Jennings's khaki-colored eyes, he knew the war of words wasn't worth sacrificing the chance to start fresh with this woman. A woman who'd stirred something deep inside him from the moment they'd met.

Chapter Five

She couldn't help but feel his hurt as she balanced Kayla's bottom on her left arm and unlocked the door. She'd always known Mrs. Applewhite to be cranky, even rude at times, but what she'd said to Tate went way beyond rude.

Phoebe pushed the door open and moved aside, gesturing toward the front hallway with her free hand. "Please, come in."

Tate's face, still red from his public flogging, stretched into a tentative smile as he nodded and stepped into the foyer, his head moving from side to side, taking in the room.

Quietly, she pushed the door closed behind her, wincing when it clicked shut. Fortunately, Kayla didn't notice.

"I'll be right back. I just want to put her down." Phoebe climbed the steps, keenly aware of Tate Williams's eyes following her as she went, her mind whirling as to the reason for his visit. Had she left something at the party? Dropped something?

She couldn't imagine what it would be. But whether she had or she hadn't, she couldn't ignore one tiny fact;

she was glad to see him. Despite his unreadable personality there was something about the man that got to her, made her think about being with someone again one day—a notion she'd dismissed from her mind the day Doug had abandoned her and their child.

For just a moment, she lingered by Kayla's crib, looking down at the eleven-month-old child who had turned her life around the moment she'd arrived. Suddenly, Doug's betrayal had faded into the background, Kayla taking front and center, evoking more joy and happiness than Phoebe had ever thought possible.

Kissing the tip of her index finger, she lowered it to Kayla's lips, felt the tug in her heart as they came together in a sucking motion. "I love you, baby girl," she whispered as she tiptoed into the hallway, leaving the nursery door slightly ajar.

When she returned to the foyer, Tate was still standing there, his face a normal color, his smile genuine and relaxed. "It's been a long time since I stood in this hallway. It feels strange and wonderful all at the same time."

Phoebe watched him for a moment. "It's sure different from where you live now, huh?"

He nodded slowly, his eyes closing briefly. "In so many ways."

She didn't know what to say, wasn't sure exactly what he meant or if he even wanted a response. Instead, she offered him a drink.

"Sounds great, Phoebe, thanks."

She led the way into the kitchen, the scent of Tate's aftershave making it difficult to think of *anything* much less what drink options she had in the house. For the past two years she'd done little else besides mourn her grandmother, lick her relationship wounds, care for Kayla and struggle to make ends meet. Men and relationships had been the last thing on her mind.

She'd given her love and trust once. And it had been tossed back in her face… Not because of who she was on the inside, but because of a role she might not be able to play convincingly enough. As if love and honor and loyalty were traits one could purchase if necessary, while throwing elegant parties and coordinating one's outfits were attainable only through bloodlines.

Her attraction to Tate Williams was purely physical—like the first sighting of water after trekking through the desert. But just because the view was alluring didn't mean she needed a drink. In fact, she'd gotten rather used to dehydration and her body had adjusted quite nicely.

She pulled the refrigerator door open and surveyed its contents. Apple juice, *check*. Whole milk, *check*. Infant cold medicine, *check*.

"It's not looking good in here, I'm afraid. Just goes to show how rusty my hostess skills have become." She nudged aside a blue-capped pitcher and pointed at a long white carton. "Now, if you have a penchant for the lactose-free milk my neighbors all drink, we're in luck."

His laugh started deep in his chest, a wonderfully rich sound that seemed to echo through the room, bringing a smile to her own lips. But it was the feel of his warm hand on her shoulder that allowed her body to relax.

"I think I'll go ahead and pass on the golden oldies drink, but I'll take a glass of water if it's okay."

She turned to face him, the cold refrigerator air bringing a chill to her bare legs, a sensation she welcomed as a way to counteract the lingering heat from his unexpected touch. "Um. Water. O-kay. I can do that."

Pushing the fridge door shut, she maneuvered around him to the sink, noting how his gaze swept across her pale pink T-shirt and white denim shorts. The naked longing she saw in his eyes both surprised and rattled her, making it difficult to think of anything, much less where she kept the glasses.

Funny, but she was suddenly thirsty. Quite thirsty.

"So much for the allure of dehydration," she mumbled as she yanked open one cabinet after the other, feeling more foolish and desperate with each passing second.

"Excuse me?"

Uh-oh.

She waved her hand in the air. "Don't mind me. Just babbling."

"Did you move things around?"

Phoebe looked over her shoulder as she opened a third cabinet. "What?"

"You're looking for glasses, right?"

She gulped. "I, uh, no. I was looking to see if I had any lemonade mix I could offer."

He lifted his hands in the air. "Really. Plain water is great. Preferable, in fact."

When she finally located the glasses she filled two with ice water and handed one to Tate. He winked at her and pointed up at the wall. "Nice border."

Grateful for the chance to take control of her emotions, she nodded. "I loved it the moment I laid eyes on it. The Realtor was going through all the things I could do with this room, and the whole time she was talking I knew I wasn't going to change a thing. The hand-painted hearts and flowers bring a warmth and sense of family that no wallpaper ever could."

He raised his glass to her and took a long sip. When he finally spoke, his voice was soft and low. "Warmth. Family. That's what my mom intended. And she spent a lot of hours trying to get it just right."

Phoebe felt her mouth gape open. "Your mom painted this?"

"She sure did," he said proudly. "Took her weeks to finish it, but she was always a perfectionist. I'm just shocked to see it's still here. You're at least the second owner since she di—well, since she's been gone."

A hint of sadness flashed across his expression as he dropped his head and trained his focus on the glass in his hand. Instinctively, Phoebe reached out and touched his arm, hoped the gesture would bring the sparkle back to his soft brown eyes. "Your mom was a talented artist, then. Her fine detail work is amazing. I've spent many hours admiring it over the past six months."

It was true. She had. In some ways his mother's work had even served as an inspiration on days when she wondered if she'd ever make it with her own art.

She told him that.

When he placed his free hand over hers and gave it a gentle squeeze, she held her breath. She was afraid that if she moved, if she spoke, the closeness she felt at that moment would disappear with a poof.

"That portrait of Shane and his family is stunning. You are a talented artist. A *very* talented artist." He set his water glass down on the counter and removed her hand from his arm, holding it in his own instead. "I can't even begin to explain how sorry I am to have assumed you were a house painter. I don't know where that came from. Ignorance, I guess." He kept his eyes locked with hers as he continued. "My mother would've given it to me good if she'd heard me last night."

Phoebe tried to laugh but his apology, coupled with the warmth of his touch and his obvious sincerity, was more than she could take at the moment.

"It's *my* fault," she answered. "That first day, at your house…I should have corrected you then about my profession. But I didn't. And your offer to help me find work? It was very thoughtful. I'm sorry."

She gently removed her hand from his and wrapped it around her glass, finding the intensity between them more than a little overwhelming. The feelings swirling in the pit of her stomach were both foreign and familiar all at the same time.

"Why didn't you correct me that first day?"

She shrugged. "I didn't think it mattered."

His gaze held hers for a long moment, as if he were trying to unearth something inside her. "It doesn't. Work is work. The world needs craftsmen just as much as they need CEOs. Probably even more so."

She shifted from foot to foot, unsure of what to say. On one hand, she wanted to question his words, challenge him. On the other, she couldn't ignore the sincerity in his voice or the way it made her throat tighten.

Tate Williams was a tough one to figure out.

"But more than that, you have an amazing gift as a painter. You should be proud of it. *That's* why you should have corrected me…put me in my place."

She'd been a fool. An absolute fool. She'd branded him

unfairly because of his wealth, using Doug's preference for money and power as a reason to stereotype. And in doing so, she wasn't much better than Kayla's father.

"I'm sorry," she repeated sincerely. Her regret and shame were threatening to erupt in a flood of tears if she didn't change the subject fast. "Would you like to sit for a little while?"

If he noticed the way her voice broke as she pointed toward the sitting room, he didn't let on. And she was grateful. He'd struck something in her—something deep and primal that she couldn't ignore.

She followed him, deliberately choosing the single chair instead of the cozy love seat he'd claimed. There was just so much temptation she could take at the moment without making a complete fool of herself.

"I'm sorry about what Mrs. Applewhite said outside. It was out of line." Phoebe dropped her hands into her lap and twisted them together. "I know there's bad blood between all of you, but maybe—"

"That's an understatement." Tate raised his own hands into the air, clasping them together before bringing them down to cradle the back of his head. "Though it's bogus. I hope you realize that."

She looked at him questioningly.

"Do you know *why* they hate me so much? What I did *wrong* to become the black sheep of Quinton Lane?"

Phoebe glanced down at her hands and then back up at Tate, her desire to answer truthfully tempered with her inability to knowingly hurt people. "I know some."

"Tell me." He rested his right ankle across his left leg, his head still leaning against his hands.

"Look, I don't want to get in the mid—"

"I don't want you to, either," he interrupted. "I just want to know what I did. In their eyes."

She stared at him. "You don't know?"

"I know how they made me feel. But I can't quite grasp why or how they turned on me the way they did."

"Okay…" She took a deep breath and tried to think of the nicest way to convey what she'd heard over the past six months. "You grew up here and everyone adored you. They were excited for you when you went to college to pursue your dreams of becoming an architect."

After hesitating just a moment, she continued. "When you'd finished, you abandoned your roots and the people who'd loved and supported you. Opting for greener pastures without so much as a glance backward."

The silence that followed her explanation was weighty and uncomfortable, the tension emanating from his body impossible to ignore. She'd made him mad. That was obvious. "Look, I'm just telling you what I've heard. I'm sorry."

He closed his eyes briefly then shook his head before opening them once again. "I'm not angry at you. Not at all. Their version is just so wrong. So very, very wrong."

She waited, unsure of what to say or do.

"May I?" he asked.

"You don't owe me an explanation."

"I know. But I want you to hear the truth. Let you make up your own mind about me." He unclasped his hands and dropped his foot to the ground, scooting forward in his seat so their knees touched. "The part about them being supportive of me going off to college was true. They even got together a little collection to help with my textbooks that first year. I'd grown up here, spent some of the happiest days of my childhood with these people and they meant the world to me."

Tate placed his hands on his thighs and lowered his voice slightly, the hurt resurfacing in his face as he continued. "I had every intention of coming back to Quinton Lane after I graduated. And I did, for a while. Lived downstairs while I waited for something to go on the market."

She noted the way his expression changed as he seemed to retreat into the past. "Shortly after I graduated, I landed a job. Nothing special. But a good filler position until something more interesting opened up. I was essentially a paid apprentice in Cedarville's planning department. It wasn't what I wanted long-term, but it was a way to get that golden experience all employers expect to see on your résumé."

He took a long, deep breath. "Anyway, I was working there when the city came after Les Walker's property."

Les Walker. She'd heard that name.

"Did he live next to the Haskells' house? Where the park and walking trail intersect with our sidewalk?"

Tate nodded. "Yes. The house was sitting on a pretty substantial easement—or right-of-way, if you prefer— and the city wanted the land to complete their award-winning fitness program. A program they boasted would rival that of big cities like Cincinnati and Columbus."

"They took his land?"

Again, he nodded. "There was a little-known clause in the city's charter that enabled them to purchase his land at fair market value to better the city as a whole. With or without his consent."

The gist of his story hit her like a splash of cold

water. "Whoa. Wait a minute. Mrs. Applewhite, the Haskells, the Jorgens…they expected *you* to stop it?"

The look on his face was all the confirmation she needed. "How could they honestly think you had a say?" she cried.

"Problem was, *without* consent it would have slowed the process somewhat. Suits could have been filed, heated town meetings would've taken place—the whole nine yards. But it still would've happened. It was the law."

"You lost me."

He inhaled loudly, as if trying to find the the courage to share the whole story. The good, the bad and the ugly. "I was given the task of researching the deed. I found out it was in the name of Mr. Walker's eldest son."

"And he gave consent, right?"

Nodding, Tate balled his left hand into a fist and cracked his knuckles. "I was just doing my job. I'm not the one who gave the go-ahead." He raised his fist to his mouth and exhaled against his skin. "Looking back, I guess I should have withheld that piece of information, but someone would have found it anyway."

"You were doing your job, Tate. The decision to go after it was the city's. Not yours."

"Maybe. But your neighbors thought I'd committed something akin to treason. And when I failed to stop the takeover, I was done."

"You were an apprentice, Tate."

"True. But for some reason my—I mean, *your* neighbors thought that by my mere status as a city employee, I had clout with the mayor and the zoning board."

Phoebe gasped. "But that's preposterous. What were you—twenty-two, maybe twenty-three?"

"Twenty-three."

The pain in his face made her heart ache for this man who'd been unfairly judged.

"Maybe *I* could make them understand—realize they made a mistake in holding you responsible."

"No!" The word shot from his mouth, surprising him as much as it did her based on the shock she saw in his eyes. "I'm sorry. I'm not angry at you, Phoebe. But I *tried* to explain, to make them understand. Numerous times. Again and again. But it didn't matter. They lost sight of everything they knew about me in favor of some grandiose idea they had about my power as a college graduate. Let them think what they think."

Phoebe studied him as he lowered his head into his hands once more. There was so much she wanted to say, to point out, but she remained silent. She knew about pride. And she knew the way misunderstandings could continue on an unending trail if left uncorrected.

She opened her mouth to speak but was cut short by a noise from Kayla's monitor.

Tate's head shot up, his eyes wide. "Did you hear that?"

She laughed. "It's just Kayla giving me the ten-minute warning."

His eyebrows rose in an upside-down V. "Ten minute-warning?"

"Uh-huh." Phoebe glanced at her watch and grinned. "Right on time, as a matter of fact."

He still looked puzzled.

"That noise was from a rollover, possibly a stretch. She's shaking out the cobwebs of sleep. And in about ten minutes she'll be calling for me."

His posture changed as the heaviness of their conversation dissipated. "She's a beautiful baby. It must be hard to raise a little one on your own."

"It is," Phoebe answered honestly. "But she is truly the sunshine in my days. She smiles from the moment she wakes up until she puts her head on the mattress at night. She's taught me how to be a mom and is endlessly patient when I mess it up."

"I, uh, I sorta noticed you don't wear a ring." He motioned around the room before looking back at her, his face slightly red. "And it's easy to see there's nothing real guyish anywhere. Was it hard going through a divorce so young?" He leaned forward in his seat once again, his full attention on her.

It was an odd feeling. In a nice way.

"There was no divorce because we never married."

The silence that ensued was something Phoebe should have expected. She'd had people respond that way since she'd started showing with Kayla. Yet it still hurt.

Pushing herself off her chair, she walked to the window that overlooked the hedge of chrysanthemums on the south side of her home. Part of her wanted to end the conversation right there, to let him think what he wanted. But to do so would be to give in to the pride he, too, needed to abandon.

She parted the white sheer curtain enough to peer outside, and offered Tate the truth, straight up. "Doug and I dated in college. Only he went to the Ivy League school on the other side of town. He was from money. I was not."

She leaned her forehead against the glass, reveled in the coolness against her skin. "We continued dating after college, though we were both busy trying to establish our grown-up lives. I'd met his family a few times, but they weren't at all approving of my blue-collar background."

Tate snorted.

"My grandmother warned me it would be an issue, that I was going to get my heart broken…but I didn't listen. Then when she died—"

Phoebe choked back the sob that threatened to spring from her throat, squeezed her eyes shut as she heard Tate's footsteps move in her direction. "I was devastated. My grandmother was the only family I had. Doug tried to comfort me. He was there for me. And it helped. Somewhat. Then I became pregnant with Kayla. It wasn't what we'd planned, of course, but we'd always talked about getting married."

She could feel Tate's breath on the back of her head and she inhaled slowly. "But talking and doing were apparently two different things. And, well, here I am. A single mom."

A lone tear escaped from each eye as Tate's hand gripped her shoulder and turned her around to face him. "You're doing a great job. All anyone has to do is look at Kayla to know that."

Phoebe closed her eyes as he cupped her face and used his thumbs to gently wipe away the wetness. She tried to speak, to say something, but as her lips parted he drew her in for a kiss. A sweet, gentle touch that made her knees weaken and her heart pound. Never in all her life had she felt the kind of intensity that was winding its way through her body at that moment. An experience she wanted to last forever—

"Ma-ma."

Or until Kayla woke up.

Slowly Phoebe pulled back to see his eyes meeting hers and a smile lighting his face. "I guess the ten minutes are up, huh?" he murmured.

"I—I have to…" She knew what she wanted to say, knew what she needed to do, but it was as if her ability to act intelligently had shut off the moment he pulled her into his arms.

He gestured toward the hallway. "I know. I'll wait. I'd like to see that sweet face again."

She glanced over her shoulder as she approached the stairs, smiled shyly at the man whose taste still lingered on her lips. There was a lot to think about. To consider and digest.

The connection she felt to Tate Williams at that moment was both surprising and wonderful all at the same time. The man he'd allowed her to see today was nothing like the man her neighbors had portrayed. Or the one she'd wrongly assumed him to be based on where he lived.

Proof once again that misunderstandings, left unchecked, were capable of unbelievable destruction and heartache.

IF HE KNEW FOR SURE the baby monitor wasn't a two-way gadget, he'd have given in to the impulse to let out a yell in celebration.

For the first time in a week he'd finally managed to get through a conversation with Phoebe without drowning in his own stupidity or shooting himself in the foot. That alone was a step in the right direction.

But the kiss? Well, that was an unexpected thrill on so many levels. Sure, he'd thought about it, even daydreamed about it many times, but to have the gumption to actually do it?

Unbelievable.

Phoebe's voice wafted down the stairs, its happy lilt widening the smile on his face as he looked around the meticulously kept room. The furnishings were different and the colors lighter, but the overall effect wasn't far removed from what his mother had achieved a decade earlier. Only here—in Phoebe's house— there was no daily infusion of negativity, no mood-zapping coldness.

The sound of footsteps interrupted his thoughts. Turning, he moved into the hallway, anxious to see Phoebe's face once more. She'd been gone less than five minutes yet he was eager to see her again. Her long, bare legs descending the staircase only upped the desire.

Kayla popped her pale yellow pacifier out of her mouth and grinned at him from the safety of her mother's arms. *"I—I—I."*

"I—I—I," he repeated, his face scrunched up like a pirate.

"Um, we haven't gotten to the pirate books yet. 'I' is just Kayla's way of saying hi." Phoebe brushed a kiss on her daughter's temple, then set her on the ground.

He laughed. "Oh. Missed that one. Well…then hi yourself, Kayla."

The baby giggled and took off, crawling furiously toward the kitchen. "Where's she going in such a hurry?"

"To find Boots." Phoebe followed her around the corner, motioning for him to follow. "It's her first postnap escapade every day."

"Do they *make* boots for feet that little?"

Phoebe stared at him, the corner of her mouth twitching.

"Seriously, do they?"

"Boo! Boo!"

Tate looked down as a flash of something orange-and-white shot past him and into the hallway, Kayla crawling after it at lightning speed.

"Boots?" he asked sheepishly.

"Boots." Phoebe pulled the dish towel from the handle of the oven door and playfully hit him in the arm.

Tate grabbed it and turned it back on her. She squealed and ran into the hallway, the physical similarity between mother and baby startling. Kayla's hair was lighter, but their eyes were almost the exact same hue, and their smile started in the same place.

It had been ages since he'd felt this carefree, this happy. And he didn't want to screw it up again.

Carefully, he returned the dish towel to its spot and headed in the direction Kayla and Phoebe had gone. He found them in the hallway, looking out the front window together, an irritated Boots watching warily from a few feet away.

"I bet Kayla's a big hit around here." Tate stopped beside them, tried to see what was so fascinating while resisting the urge to drape an arm across Phoebe's shoulder. He didn't want to push it too far, too fast.

She bounced her daughter on her hip. "Oh, she is. They adore her. It's like having five or six different grandparents around at any given time."

A pair of tiny arms shot out in his direction, brushing him on the shoulder.

"She wants you to hold her," Phoebe said with a sparkle in her eye.

"Gladly." He put his hands under the baby's arms and pulled her to him, blowing softly against her cheek before looking at Phoebe once again. "Hey, what was going on next door when I arrived? The whole street seemed to be there."

"They were. I feel bad for them. They want desperately to hold on to that land." Phoebe stepped back from the window and leaned against the antique table, her long, slender legs claiming his attention once again.

He swallowed hard, forced himself to focus on something besides Phoebe's legs and how it would feel to have them wrapped around him. "What land?"

"The green space."

He caught the baby's pudgy hand in his as it made its way up to his mouth. "What's wrong with the green space?"

Phoebe waved in the air. "Apparently, if we don't come up with a way to beautify the space in some unique way, the city is going to take it over and turn it into a citywide park."

He stared at her. "They can't do tha—wait, strike that. They can. And they have. As you now know." He turned Kayla around to face the outdoors, his left arm under her bottom, his right hand supporting her calves. "But why? Why would they want it?"

Phoebe shrugged, her eyebrows rising. "It's part of their Clean Up Cedarville campaign."

"But that land has belonged to Quinton Lane for decades."

He watched as she brought her palms to her face and

exhaled. "I know. And trust me, we're trying to come up with anything we can to hang on to it."

"Such as?" Kayla squirmed in his arms and he shot a question in Phoebe's direction. At her nod, he set the little girl down, Boots disappearing once again, Kayla in hot pursuit.

"I don't know yet. Right now we're just trying to figure out how to raise funds so we have a chance. You know these people. They have no money."

He peered out the window once again, his attention settling on the two or three houses he could see from where he stood. Homes that held the secrets of all who'd lived there. But the green space had always been the one place where the people of Quinton Lane had come together. For birthday parties, graduation ceremonies, summer picnics and winter bonfires. A simple, yet perfect place that had been the backdrop for the kind of memories people held dear. Including him.

And while he would never consider living on or around Quinton Lane again, that didn't mean he could forget the good times he'd had here while growing up. Or the role the green space had played in fostering them.

"Tate?"

Phoebe's soft, tentative voice broke through his woolgathering and he turned to face her. He'd give anything to continue their kiss, to slide his hands down her arms, to feel her breasts in his hands. But the reappearance of Kayla made that difficult. As did a desire to keep from being thrown out on his ear.

"I found an address for your father so Kayla and I are going to pay him a visit today. To deliver his letter." She reached behind her back and plucked the envelope from its perch against the table-mounted mirror. "I'd gotten so wrapped up in finishing the portrait that I wasn't able to deliver it any sooner. Now that I'm done, I want to make sure to get it to him. We'd love to have you come with us. I could even make some dinner afterward if you like spagh—"

"No! Absolutely not!" His words reverberated through the foyer with a fury he didn't intend, yet couldn't control. An intense outburst riled only by the subsequent sound of Kayla's frightened cry.

Chapter Six

It had taken every ounce of willpower Phoebe possessed to push Tate Williams out of her thoughts. And it still hadn't worked. Not really, anyway.

He was there as she printed up directions to the Garden View Retirement Village. He was there as she slipped a pale yellow sundress on Kayla and pulled her hair into two tiny pigtails. And he was still there now, as she stopped at the visitor's desk for a guest pass to meet his father.

The kiss alone was hard to forget, but it was more than that. He'd been so compassionate when she'd shared her background with Doug, so open when he'd spoken of the rift with her neighbors and the hurt that still remained. And he'd gone out of his way to apologize for comments that weren't even entirely his fault.

Yet the notion of visiting his father was so incredibly appalling he'd scare her baby half to death then walked out the door with barely a look backward.

"Men."

"You can say that again."

Phoebe froze, her mental cloud clearing as she

looked around the desk for a person to go with the voice. "Excuse me?"

"I'm sorry. I don't usually make a habit of eavesdropping on our guests. But your voice, and what you said just now—well, I get it. Boy, do I get it." A college student sporting a white T-shirt with a big yellow smiley face pointed at her name tag. "I'm Jeannie. How can I help you? Short of eliminating the offending gender, of course."

Kayla reached out and waved her hand wildly, her pint-size squeal echoing through the two-story atrium.

Jeannie nodded, her expression serious despite the glint in her eye. "That's right, little one. Save yourself the trouble and just stay away from all men. Who needs 'em, anyway? Well, except maybe for…well, that…"

Phoebe's lips twitched. "I'm not entirely convinced they're even worth *that*." She rested Kayla's bottom on the countertop as she extended her free hand toward the receptionist. "I'm Phoebe Jennings and this is Kayla. I called earlier this morning to see if it would be possible to pay a visit to one of your residents—Mr. Bart Williams."

A quick scrunch of her eyebrows was followed by a tap of her pen on the desk. "Right. I remember. Here… take this." She handed a green laminated index card to Phoebe, then wrote something in a small green book beside her desk phone. "It lets security know that you've checked in and have permission to be in our independent living wing."

"Independent living?" Phoebe asked.

The girl nodded. "Residents in that section of our village are simply senior citizens who'd rather live in this type of setting as opposed to a more traditional apartment complex. Less noise. More opportunity for making friends. And the peace of mind that comes with knowing you're in a safe place."

"I see." Phoebe gave the card to Kayla and lifted her into her arms once again. "Thanks, Jeannie. Now which way do I—"

The girl stepped out from behind her desk and motioned down the long hallway. "Take this all the way to the end, then turn right. Mr. Williams's apartment is at the end of that second hallway. You can't miss his flag."

Kayla waved bye-bye as Phoebe headed in the direction indicated. They hadn't gone more than ten feet when Jeannie called out to them one last time. "I'm glad you're here to see Mr. Williams. He seems awful lonely and I think that baby of yours will make his day."

Phoebe could only hope that was true. Her day was in desperate need of a few more smiles and a lot less drama.

A featherlight kiss on her jawbone brought her back to the moment, visions of hostile neighbors and cranky architects disappearing in a poof. She glanced down at Kayla and grinned. "Thank you, sweetie. That makes Mommy happiest of all." And it was true. As hard as it was to be a single mother with limited backup support, it was all worth it to have Kayla in her world. Aside from the happy smiles and sweet kisses, her daughter had taught her so much about life.

And about herself.

It *was* okay to have dreams. To believe in your ability to reach them. And to know that there could never be a monetary amount that would make her give them up. Ever.

Phoebe donned her best conspiratorial tone and widened her eyes as she looked at Kayla. "Are you ready to deliver our letter?"

"Da."

"That's my girl."

At the end of the first hallway they turned right, finding a massive dining room visible through the first doorway. A dozen or so circular tables were scattered throughout the space, each one covered with a white linen tablecloth and a miniature wicker wheelbarrow filled with the colors of summer. The bright yellow daisies, purple and pink lilacs, and white daylilies looked fresh from the garden, waiting to be admired by the dinner crowd.

The second door opened to a small beauty parlor, both chairs occupied by white-haired women getting dolled up. One of the women was passing a photograph to her stylist while proudly announcing she was a grand-mother for the tenth time.

Phoebe cuddled Kayla closer and forced herself to focus on the wall-mounted flag at the end of the hall. The last thing she needed to do was show up at Bart Williams's door with tears running down her face. But oh, what she wouldn't give to see her grandmother one more time. To hold her hand. To hug her. To watch the joy in her eyes as she held her only great-grandchild for the very first time....

"Oh, Tate, you've got to find a way to make things right with your dad." Her whispered words made Kayla peer up at her and happily wave the green visitor card in the air.

"You're right, sweetie. We're here to deliver a letter, not to play mediator in a dispute we know nothing about. And besides, I've had my share of unyielding men to last a lifetime." But even as Phoebe said the words, she knew better. Knew herself well enough to know she simply couldn't help trying to fix relationships even if much of that work was done from behind the curtain. Ironic, considering she couldn't find a way—short of selling her soul—to keep the one man she'd ever really loved.

Though, lately, she'd come to wonder whether she'd truly loved Doug. Sure, they'd had fun dating in college, but they'd been so busy after graduation that she'd actually entertained the idea of seeing other people. But when her grandmother died she'd sought comfort in the only other pair of arms she knew.

Doug's.

Yet in all the years they'd been together, he'd never evoked the kind of head-spinning passion she'd experienced for the few moments she'd been in Tate's arms. How much of that was genuine and how much was deprivation was anyone's guess.

Though she wouldn't mind an encore to find out…

"Ugh." Shaking all thoughts of Tate Williams from her mind, Phoebe stopped outside Bart Williams's room and took a deep breath, her hand moving from Kayla's back long enough to reach inside her purse and touch the letter that had brought them there in the first place.

This visit was about Bart and his letter. Nothing more and nothing less. And once she'd made her delivery, there'd be no reason ever to see him or his son again.

Squaring her shoulders, Phoebe pressed the tip of Kayla's nose gently then knocked on the white, six-panel door. Around them doors opened and faces popped out, only to disappear when their owners realized her knock wasn't for them. She tried again, this time a little bit louder.

"Who's there?" The words were muffled, yet firm, reminding Phoebe of a bark rather than a greeting.

"Mr. Williams? My name is Phoebe Jennings and I live in your old home on Quinton Lane. A letter arrived in my mailbox for you a few days ago and I—I wanted to make sure you got it."

The words were barely out of her mouth before the interior lock was disengaged and the door pulled open. Phoebe stepped back and hoisted Kayla farther up her hip, her eyes drawn to the man who looked out at them with a mixture of curiosity and pleasure.

She'd have known he was Bart Williams with or without the thin rectangular nameplate on the wall. The above-average height, the proud posture, the soft brown eyes and full head of thick hair were all features she'd seen just hours earlier on Bart's son.

Even the twinkle in the elderly man's eyes was reminiscent of Tate. Especially the way it seemed to appear just before the endearing smile that lit his face from within.

"A warm welcome to you." The man's eyes drifted from Phoebe's face to her arms. "And to you, too, young lady."

He reached a bent finger in Kayla's direction and tickled her stomach. The baby's ensuing giggle widened his smile even more.

"And to think I thought today would be like every other day. Slow and boring." Bart Williams stepped backward and motioned to his sparsely decorated studio apartment. "Please, please come in. I know the place is nothing to look at, but it suits my basic needs."

Phoebe walked inside and looked around, her gaze skimming across the alcove that housed a mini refrigerator, tabletop microwave and freestanding oak cabinet. A table for two had been pushed against the wall, making it more what it truly was—a table for one.

The spot where the white-and-tan linoleum stopped and the beige carpet began denoted the sitting room. This section was furnished with a teal-blue recliner, matching love seat and an old-fashioned tube television. The only attempt at decorating was on the room's lone end table—providing the one real glimpse into the man who lived within the apartment's four walls. It was there she finally spied a few personal mementos— two homemade 4 x 6 picture frames with snapshots she couldn't identify from where she stood, and what appeared to be a sketch, visible beneath the table's circular glass top.

She felt Tate's father studying her and turned to meet his inspection head-on. "How long have you been here?"

His shoulders drooped a hairbreadth before he recovered enough to point to the love seat. "Too long. But that doesn't matter today. *Today* I have company, so won't you please sit and stay a while?"

Although she'd only been in his presence for five minutes, it was hard for Phoebe to imagine what could possibly keep Tate from this man. What kind of disagreement was worth letting their time together as father and son disappear through their fingers?

Not your business, Phoebe. Stay out of it.

Training her focus on the reason for her visit, Phoebe perched on the edge of the love seat, lowering Kayla to the floor as Bart Williams claimed the well-worn recliner to her right. The baby sat for a moment, her eyes as big as saucers as she took in the new setting.

"What's her name?" Bart asked, his words directed at Phoebe while his eyes sparkled at the baby.

"Her name is Kayla. She's eleven months old and has shown no real interest in walking yet. She prefers to get where she's going as quickly as possible. And for now, her chosen method is crawling."

Bart nodded. "My son was like that. Didn't walk until he was almost fifteen months. But when he did…look out."

For some odd reason Phoebe suddenly felt uneasy. As if hearing things about Tate's childhood, without his consent, was underhanded in some way. Silly, perhaps. But the guilt remained.

"I…I have your letter." Phoebe reached into her purse and extracted the envelope from the center section. "I've been looking forward to getting this to you since—"

Bart waved his hand dismissively. "So, you live on Quinton Lane now, do you?"

She smiled and nodded as he settled back in his chair, a look of contentment on his face as he continued talking. "I miss that place. Home has never felt quite like it did there."

"I know what you mean. Mrs. Applewhite, and Ms. Weatherby, and Mr. Borden, and the Haskells and, well, *everyone* on that street has welcomed Kayla and me with open arms. Something we desperately needed."

The man nodded in turn and his gaze seemed to drift off to a place and conversation far away. "I could have lived my whole life there. If things had been different at the end." His voice dipped suddenly as his focus reconnected with the here and now. "Uh, don't mind me.

I'm just an old man suffering from nostalgia for people and places that are no longer."

There was something about his words and the way he said them that made Phoebe wonder if his son was included in that statement. But if he was, Bart wasn't sharing. And she wasn't about to pry.

"I plan on raising Kayla there. I have no interest or desire to live anywhere else. Ever."

His hands gently gripped the armrests of his chair as he leaned forward long enough to wiggle his fingers at Kayla before responding in a voice that seemed deliberately void of emotion. "Well, young lady, I hope nothing ever changes your mind the way it did for—" He stopped and reached for the envelope, turning it over and over in his hands. "Doesn't look like a bill, so I guess it can't be *too* bad."

Phoebe pointed at the faded red circle on the front of the envelope. "Did you see the date on the postmark? That's one very old letter you have in your hands, Mr. Williams."

She watched as he held the yellowed envelope upward, tipping it back and forth. "I lost my glasses somewhere and can't read anything that's not in big block letters. How old is this thing anyway?"

"Almost forty years."

"Fort—did you just say *forty years?*" He raised the letter close to his face, his eyes squinting as he examined it.

"That's right. Forty years." Phoebe handed her key ring down to Kayla, then looked back at Bart. "Amazing, isn't it?"

"How? I didn't live on Quinton Lane forty years ago."

"Apparently my house is the last known address they had for you."

The man nodded momentarily before asking yet another question, the disbelief in his voice offset by a twinge of curiosity. "Okay. But *why now?* Where's it been all this time?"

"I don't know, exactly. I remember reading once about a letter falling behind a table at a post office, only to be discovered ten years later. Maybe it was something like that. The apology note never said." She pushed a strand of hair from her forehead and inhaled slowly. "When I saw the name, Tate Williams, on the front, I—"

"It's addressed to *Tate?*" The letter began to shake, along with Bart Williams's hand.

"Yes, but it's okay. With the date of that postmark it can only be yours…" Her voice trailed off as the color began to drain from the elderly man's face. The cheeks that had been tinged pink with pleasure at their arrival were growing paler with each passing second. She pushed herself off the love seat and bridged the gap between them in seconds. Crouching beside the recliner, Phoebe touched his hand. "Mr. Williams, are you all right?"

His silence was punctuated only by the slow nod of his head.

"Should I get someone for you?" Phoebe glanced to the left long enough to establish a visual on Kayla before looking back at Bart.

He met her concern with a soft pat on her forearm and words so raspy she could barely make them out. "What's the original address on the letter?"

Without looking down, she recited the address

scrawled across the center of the envelope. The man's eyes slowly closed as she did so.

"Would you read it to me, please?"

"You want me to *read* your letter?"

He nodded once more as a lone tear escaped from his closed eyes.

Phoebe took the envelope from his hand and slowly slid her finger underneath the seal. The letter itself was written on real stationary, something she hadn't seen since her grandmother was alive. Phoebe carefully unfolded the letter and smoothed it against her leg, her gaze lingering on the pair of soft pink hearts tied together with a lace-trimmed ribbon at the top. Below the design was the same flowery handwriting she'd been staring at all week.

Reclaiming her spot on the sofa, she cleared her throat and began to read.

My dearest Tate,

I received your letter just a few hours ago and have spent the time since pinching myself.

The thought of becoming your wife is the most wonderful thing I could ever imagine. I have loved you from the first moment I saw you and have missed you every single second since you've been gone.

Phoebe peered up at the man in the recliner as her voice wavered. His eyes remained closed despite the addition of more tears on his cheeks. Swallowing over the sudden tightness in her throat, she looked back down and continued reading.

The second I read your letter I wanted to respond, but I did as you asked and handed the smaller envelope to my father. I am thrilled to announce that we have my parents' blessing!

But I'm even more excited to tell you that I want nothing more in this life than to be your wife. So my answer is "yes" a hundred times over.

All my love,
Your Lorraine

The final line was met with quiet sobbing, a heart-broken sound that tugged at Phoebe's heart. Not knowing what to say, she returned to his side, bending down low enough to embrace him, the shoulder of her shirt absorbing the tears that fell so freely. "I'm so sorry, Mr. Williams. If I'd known it was going to cause you so much pain I never would have given it to you."

She felt his head move against her skin as he pulled away.

"No. You did the right thing." Bart Williams pulled a tissue from his shirt pocket and blew his nose quietly. "*Not* receiving this letter caused far more hurt. At least now I know."

As darts of pain radiated up her thighs from her awkward position, Phoebe stood and managed a smile in Kayla's direction. The baby dropped the keys and crawled over, stopping at Phoebe's feet to raise her arms upward.

"May I?" Bart asked quietly. "Hold her, I mean?"

"Sure." Phoebe plucked Kayla from the ground and sat her on the elderly man's lap before fishing a small canister of Cheerios from her purse. "She'd love it if you'd hold this while she eats."

He took the cup and popped the lid open, shaking it just enough to claim Kayla's attention. The eager smile he received in return brightened his face immeasurably, though his eyes didn't lose their sadness.

Phoebe sat quietly, not wanting to interrupt any good that was coming from Kayla's innocent joy, yet sensing a distinct change in the man's demeanor since she'd read the letter aloud. But just as she began to think there would be no more conversation, Bart finally reestablished eye contact.

"Do you…" He stopped, then started again, his voice cautious and unsteady. "Do you think a broken heart can change a person so much it ruins their heart for someone else? Even when that someone else was every bit as wonderful?"

Phoebe couldn't have been more ill prepared for a question if she tried. As a result, she simply sat there, alternating between clasping her hands and picking at imaginary lint on her legs.

"I, uh—"

He held up his hand, palm outward, a hint of color finally returning to his face. "Phoebe, I'm sorry. You don't have to answer that. I didn't mean to ask it in a prying way. It's just…well, it's just—" With a shrug, he stopped talking and looked back down at Kayla. "She sure is a happy little girl."

Phoebe wanted to say something, to let him know the question was okay, yet she didn't know how to answer it. Mostly because it was something she herself wondered about. Often.

"It's not that the question was out of line," she finally said, her mind whirling, "it's just that I'm not sure how to answer it. I, too, had my heart broken on a large scale, and I'm not sure if I'll *ever* be able to give it so completely again."

She felt Bart's eyes studying her, but it didn't matter. Whatever had happened in his past, whatever went wrong between him and Tate, one thing was certain— he knew about hurt, and that alone put Phoebe and him on common ground.

"I'm sorry to hear that." He inhaled deeply, jutting his chin in Kayla's direction. "She's drifting off."

At Phoebe's agreement, the man pulled the baby closer, cuddling her into the crook of his arm. As Kayla's eyelids continued to droop, he grinned.

"That kind of innocence is something we just don't enjoy as adults." He paused for a moment, then leaned his head back against the recliner, his voice taking on a faraway quality. "I met Lorraine about six months before I left for a twelve-month deployment overseas. Although I miraculously escaped an assignment in Vietnam, my contact with home was still limited. Except for letters. And boy, did Lorraine and I write letters to each other. Daily. Sometimes two and three times a day.

"Those letters brought us closer on a level I think few achieve even when they're together day after day. She mailed me things she'd knitted—a scarf, a hat, a sweater. I'd mail her little trinkets from overseas—a postcard, pictures we had taken on days off. We fell madly in love with one another. Or…" He stopped, looked at the letter Phoebe had placed on his armrest and sighed. "Or at least I knew *I* was in love."

She pulled her legs onto the couch and settled back in turn. "You proposed in a letter?"

He nodded. "I did. I couldn't wait another moment. I had four more months left of my deployment and I wanted to become her husband as soon as I returned."

Phoebe nibbled her lower lip as she focused on Bart's story. From time to time she'd stop to ask a question, but for the most part she simply listened as the words poured from the elderly man's lips.

"But weeks turned into months and I never heard from her again. No reply to my proposal. *At all.* I figured she'd found someone else. It happened all the time to guys I was stationed with."

"But you got out four months later, right?"

His gaze dropped to a sleeping Kayla, his words filled with an anguish that broke her heart. "I was devastated, humiliated. And, as men often do, I reacted. Or, rather, acted out. I re-upped my tour. Stayed in for another four years. I began dating women overseas, never seeing any of them more than once or twice. It became a game of sorts…

"A game that didn't quit when I finally got out of the military and returned to the States. I avoided the town where Lorraine lived, convinced myself I was better off. And that was pretty much my life. Until I met Mary."

He reached out, plucked one of the frames from the end table beside his recliner and studied it for a few silent moments before holding it out to Phoebe. She took it, swinging her feet back to the ground. The woman in the picture was breathtaking in a girl-next-door kind of way. Her hair, which seemed to be blond despite the black-and-white photograph, was shoulder-length. The smile on her face accentuated her high cheekbones and the almond shape of her eyes.

"Is this Mary?" she asked, realizing before he even answered that she was looking at the woman who'd painted the border in her kitchen.

Tate's mother.

"Yes. That's Mary. She changed something in me when we met. It was like she flipped a switch that had turned off when Lorraine failed to acknowledge my proposal. I felt something. Something real. Something powerful. Eventually we married." His words petered out for a brief moment as he closed his eyes. "Mary was a tremendous woman. The kind of spouse everyone dreams about. I had her, I had the perfect wife…yet I didn't appreciate her like I should have. And I think that's because there was a part of me that could never quite forget Lorraine or her rejection. A part that always wondered what happened, and—I'm ashamed to admit—a part that wondered what if. What if she'd said yes? What if we'd married? What would my life have been like? That sort of thing."

Phoebe sat there motionless, yet again not sure what to say. Fortunately she didn't have to worry as Bart continued with words he seemed to need to hear as much as he needed to speak them. "As a result, I wasn't always the best husband. I wasn't appreciative of all the things Mary did. And because I felt lousy about myself inside, I seemed to have this need to hold her down—her dreams, her hopes."

Phoebe's stomach tightened as her mind began replaying the animosity in Tate's voice whenever his father was mentioned. The story she was hearing was surely a contributing factor to that anger. And as the man continued, she couldn't help but wish she'd reacted differently to Tate's outburst that morning. Perhaps if she'd known some of this earlier, she might have been more sympathetic and a little less offended.

But she hadn't known. And she certainly hadn't cut him any slack.

So much for trying to fix things all the time…

"I think I had so many unanswered questions and so much pent-up frustration—even anger—that I held a part of myself back. As if I was punishing Mary for Lorraine's betrayal…or what I *thought* was her betrayal. Or maybe, somehow, I was so afraid of being rejected again that I kept a wall up at all times, even when my heart craved Mary and her love."

He propped his elbow on the armrest and lowered his forehead to his hand. "I've spent many sleepless nights looking back. Regretting the hurt I invariably caused my family. And now," he murmured, his voice quavering, "I realize, had I received this when it was mailed, I would have married Lorraine. I never would have met Mary. And Mary could have had the opportunity to find someone void of all the baggage I brought to our marriage. Someone who would have *shown* her how deeply she was loved."

He stopped speaking, regret filling the silent space as if it were a living, breathing presence. They sat like that for what seemed like ages before Phoebe finally spoke, her words quiet yet steady.

"If I've learned anything from my broken heart it's that all things happen for a reason. I think, for me, it was better we didn't stay together, from the simple standpoint that Doug was wrong for me. He would have sucked the joy right out of my life." She stood and walked over to the end table that had held Mary's picture. "Yet, had I not met him, I wouldn't have Kayla."

With barely a glance to confirm her suspicion, she plucked the remaining frame from its spot on the table and handed it to Bart. "Had that letter arrived when it should have, you'd have married Lorraine. And if you had, you wouldn't have—"

The quiet sobbing began again, the sound even more gut wrenching and heartfelt than before. But no matter how hard it was for him to speak through the sudden flood of emotion, he managed to find the words to complete her sentence.

"If I'd married Lorraine…I wouldn't have my son."

Chapter Seven

It didn't take a genius to know the design he'd been working on for the past hour was pure garbage. The entrance was boring, the window placement was off and the building as a whole looked as if he'd drawn it in his sleep. While being chased by aliens.

Tate Williams flung his pencil into the canister at the top of his drafting table and reclined back in his chair until he was staring at the ceiling. It was a view he'd sought often over the past forty-eight hours, a neutral backdrop for the one image that kept playing over and over in his brain. A reminder of his overwhelming stupidity.

"Good morning, boss."

If storming out of Phoebe's house like a toddler with a serious case of the terrible twos wasn't bad enough, he'd actually—

"Boss?"

"Huh?" With a slight heave forward, Tate's gaze left the ceiling in favor of the office door he could've sworn he'd closed. "What *is* it, Regina?"

Even if he hadn't come to during his last few words, he'd have known his tone was snarky simply by the way his secretary's eyebrows furrowed in surprise. He felt even worse as she held up her hand and backed away, a twinge of hurt in her eyes.

"I'm sorry. I knocked, but you didn't answer."

"Wait!" Tate jumped to his feet and jogged over to the door. "Come in. Sit. Smack me. Curse me. Whatever. I deserve it. All of it."

"As tempting as that sounds, you have a visitor." She pushed the door shut behind her and lowered her voice. "I know you're preparing for your meeting with the partners, but I get the sense this might be important."

He shook his head as he peered over at his desk, to the file he was supposed to be compiling for his lunch meeting. "Take a phone number and I'll get back to him. I'm not in a terribly personable mood at the moment and I really need to focus. This could be the day, Regina."

"No *could* about it, boss." She turned on her sensible heels and reached for the doorknob. "I'll let Miss Jennings know."

His head snapped up as his secretary's words broke through his mental cloud. "Did you say *Jennings?*"

"Yes. Sweet girl. And very pretty, too."

With a shove of his hand he thwarted Regina's attempt to open the door. "She's here?" he whispered.

"Uh-huh. Right outside."

Cupping his hand to his mouth, he exhaled deeply. He'd acted like a total idiot over the weekend, yet she'd still sought him out—

"Did she have a shotgun, by any chance?"

Regina's brows furrowed. "Boss?"

"Never mind. How about a baby?"

Confusion gave way to awareness as his secretary shook her head. "This is the one with the letter, isn't it?"

He looked around the office, at the countless awards and photographs documenting his success. Accomplishments he suspected were about to lead him to the role of partner as early as that afternoon. But somehow it all paled before the notion of seeing Phoebe Jennings once again.

"Give me two minutes and then send her in, okay?"

Regina's eyes sparkled. "Yes, boss."

Drawing a deep breath, he strode around the room, his foul mood a thing of the past. He knew he needed to apologize for his outburst Saturday morning, and then he hoped they could move forward. Quickly.

The feelings she'd ignited in him as they'd kissed were ones he wanted to explore further. All the way to the bedroom if she'd let him.

He stopped in front of the window and looked down over Morgan Lake. His view was one of the best in the building, and he took advantage of it often as a way to detox after a particularly stressful project or client. The morning sun reflecting off the surface of the water warmed him where he stood, and he couldn't help but imagine holding Phoebe Jennings in his arms in the very same spot.

"Tate?"

At the sound of her soft voice he turned, his eyes drawn to the woman standing in the partially open doorway. Phoebe shifted nervously, drawing his eye to where the hem of her classy white linen skirt hit just below midthigh. She'd pulled her hair back with a clip, leaving thin tendrils to frame her delicate features. He felt his body stir with awareness.

"Phoebe, it's good to see you." He closed the distance between them in several quick strides, reaching for her hand and giving it a gentle, lingering squeeze.

"I did a little digging and found out where you work. I hope you don't mind me showing up like this. I won't stay long."

"No, please. It's a nice surprise. Come in. Sit down." He gestured toward the small sitting area in the back right corner of the room. "I've been thinking about our time together. A lot."

He followed her to the pair of armchairs he often used during first visits with a new client. The more relaxed atmosphere tended to nurture creativity. Today, though, his creative energy wasn't focused on blueprints and sketches. Phoebe Jennings was the only thing that stoked his curiosity and imagination. That and the gnawing desire to explore the sensuous curves of her slender body.

Phoebe stopped just short of the vacant chairs and turned around, her eyes void of the sparkle he remembered. "I've been thinking about it a lot, as well, and I'm sorry. I was out of line, sticking my nose where it didn't belong. I hope you'll forgive me." She looked down at her hands, linked them together nervously. "I knew from the first afternoon we met that there was bad blood between you and your father. I should have left it alone. I should have—"

"Hey." He nudged her chin upward with his fingers until their eyes met. "I shouldn't have snapped like I did. You were just trying to be nice."

Her eyes searched his closely and he smiled in response. "You are a beautiful woman, Phoebe Jennings."

A hint of red arose in her cheeks as she looked down. "Thank you."

"No, thank *you*." Without thinking, he released her chin to brush a lock of hair from her cheek, the feel of her skin beneath his fingertips igniting his desire even more. "Where's Kayla this morning?"

"Mrs. Haskell agreed to watch her for an hour. I thought about bringing her, but didn't know how you'd react to seeing me."

His gut twisted in guilt as memories of his weekend outburst came flooding back. "Look, Phoebe, I'm sorry I exploded the way I did. I'm not prone to temper tantrums like that, I swear."

She didn't reply. Instead, she turned her head and looked slowly around the room. "I saw the photographs on the wall out in the hall. Your secretary said you designed every one of those buildings."

"I did."

"They're amazing."

"Thank you." He'd always been proud of his work and his accomplishments, but hearing praise from Phoebe took it to a level he'd never expected.

"May I?" She gestured toward the built-in bookshelves lining the east wall of his office. Shelves that housed the many plaques and awards he'd received since coming to McDonald and Murphy.

"Of course." He resisted the urge to follow, opting instead to admire her from afar. And admire he did. Every. Single. Little. Detail.

"Tate?"

Uh-oh. He'd missed something…

"I'm sorry, Phoebe. What was that?"

She pointed at the assortment of ribbon-cutting photographs that graced the top shelf. "These are special."

"Yes, they are. Pictorial evidence of a completed job."

Phoebe nodded softly. "I know that party the other night wasn't about the family portrait I'd painted, but seeing it on the wall was so special, so exciting. I wish I'd snapped a picture of it hanging there."

"I know Shane pretty well. I'm sure he'd let us go take one."

"It's okay. I have one right here," she said, pointing to her heart. "I just wish my grandmother could have been there to see it, too."

"She was."

His heart ached with tenderness as those green eyes focused on his face. "You think so?"

"Yeah, I do. That kind of love, that kind of connection doesn't just disappear. It's too precious." Keeping his eyes on hers, he closed the distance between them. Never in his life had he had such an urge to touch a woman, to hold her close. And he wasn't about to let this chance pass.

Pulling her against him, he simply held her, reveled in the feel of her soft body molded to his. "I'm glad you stopped by," he murmured, the sensation of her hair beneath his lips creating an undeniable reaction in his body. "I missed doing this—"

Gently, deliberately, Tate guided Phoebe's mouth to his own, sought the warmth and softness he'd experienced just days earlier. She parted her lips in response, allowing him to explore her mouth with his tongue.

He dropped his hands from her shoulders and grasped her hips, pulling her still closer as his mouth sought her neck, her ear...

"Your door is open," she whispered.

"No, it's—" He looked up, silently cursed the reality. "Missed that detail."

"It's okay." She pressed her palms against his chest and stepped back, then smoothed her hair. "Your secretary told me you had a meeting in a little while so I don't want to keep you."

He groaned. Any other day he'd be climbing the walls in anticipation of a lunch meeting with his boss—particularly when his future with the company was the expected topic. But not today. Today he wanted to lose himself in this woman.

"You have a really important job, don't you?" she asked quietly.

"I guess."

She looked back at the pictures on the shelves, an open scrapbook of his life—both at work and play. "Do you attend many parties like the one Mr. Dolanger threw?"

"All the time."

"Not many barbecues, I imagine." Her voice grew ever quieter as she stepped closer to the second set of shelves.

He laughed. "No. Galas are more likely. Most of the parties I attend—or host—are on a different scale than a backyard barbecue."

"I see."

"Caterers are hired, bands are brought in, the best wines served."

"Sounds like a foreign country to me." She continued her inspection of the photographs, stopping when she reached the one in the center of the middle shelf. "This is your mother, isn't it?"

"Yes, it is."

"She's a little older in this picture, yet every bit as beautiful."

"Older?"

Phoebe nodded. "In the one I saw she was closer to my age."

"How did you see...?" His voice trailed off as confusion morphed into understanding.

The letter.

"Your father loved your mother very much," Phoebe said softly, her gaze leaving the photograph and coming to rest on his face.

"That man wouldn't know love if it jumped in his lap," Tate growled, anger and frustration coursing through his body. Fisting his hands at his sides, he walked to the window, stared unseeingly at the lake below. "You show up at his door touting some nonsense letter, and you think that means you know him? That *you* can tell *me* what my life was like as a kid? You're crazy, absolutely craz—"

"She's gone, boss."

HE SET HIS BRIEFCASE down on his desk long enough to open it and remove the Dolanger file. The extended lunch with the bosses had gone amazingly well, and barring any unforeseen circumstances, the sign in the lobby would be changing to McDonald, Murphy and Williams very soon.

Making partner at his age was an accomplishment all on its own. Making partner in a firm as prestigious as McDonald and Murphy was even more impressive.

Yet now that Tate's dream had finally come true, he wasn't as enamored by the notion as he'd expected. And he knew why.

Phoebe Jennings.

Somehow, some way, the woman who had shown up on his doorstep simply looking to deliver a misplaced letter had captured his heart as no one ever had before. She made him laugh, think, feel, imagine and believe.

The laughter had been easy. Her beautiful smile and sweet innocence would make anyone come alive. Her selfless nature caused him to think, to examine himself in ways he hadn't in years. Seeing how she loved her daughter brought up welcome memories from his own childhood. Her willingness to share her past and to forgive so easily made him imagine that, one day, he could find something similar in himself.

But above all, there was something about her that made him believe a happily ever after could exist— between the right people.

A soft knock at the door interrupted his thoughts and he turned, his gaze coming to rest on Regina's wide smile.

"I hear congratulations are in order." She stepped into his office, closing the door behind her. "You've worked so hard for this partnership, and I couldn't be happier for you than I am at this moment."

Shrugging, he leaned against his desk and ran a hand through his hair. "Yeah. Pretty cool, isn't it?"

He felt her studying him and looked up to meet her eyes. "What?" he growled.

"May I?" She pointed at the chair opposite his desk. When he nodded, she perched on the edge, ready to resume her duties at the ring of a phone or the sound of a footstep. "The day I interviewed with you, you told me you wanted to be partner. It's been your one motivating goal the past few years. Yet now that it's here, you don't seem terribly excited."

He couldn't argue, because she was dead-on in her assessment. Still, he offered nothing more than a shrug of agreement.

Regina shifted on the edge of the chair, clasping and unclasping her hands. The one time she started to speak ended with her clamping her lips shut before a single word was spoken.

"Say what's on your mind. *Please.*" Tate crossed his ankles as he waited.

After a few moments of silence this woman whom he'd come to rely on in ways that went far beyond secretarial expertise spoke, each word carefully chosen. "It's this Phoebe Jennings, isn't it? She's touched something in you."

He exhaled a breath he didn't know he was holding, buoyed by the knowledge that someone other than himself sensed what had been playing with his emotions for days. "Yeah. She has. I've spent a grand total of about an hour with this woman in the past week and she's all I can think about. Day and night. Night and day. I've never felt like this, Regina."

"What's your gut telling you?"

Tate braced his hands on the edge of the desk. There were so many things about Regina he appreciated, but none more than her ability to make him think on a deeper level. He considered her question, the answer coming surprisingly quickly. "I think *she's* the reason I haven't had many second dates."

Regina cocked her head to the side. "Go on."

"My mom used to tell me that when the right person

came along, I'd know it. I'd feel something different.
And—" He stopped, suddenly feeling foolish.

"And you think Phoebe might be the one," Regina
finished in a soft voice.

"Yeah."

For a moment neither of them spoke, each absorbed
in their own thoughts. Finally, she broke the silence, her
words hitting Tate with a force he hadn't expected.

"Then you have some soul searching to do. Some
choices you have to make."

He felt his eyebrows dip downward. "Choices?"

She nodded, her hands clasped in her lap. "As long
as you hold grudges you will never be free to love
completely."

He crossed his arms in front of his chest and waited
for her to continue.

Her face reddening ever so slightly, Regina said, even
more quietly than before, "I saw the look on your face
when you realized Phoebe was here. It was impossible
to miss. Yet you let your anger toward your father ruin
a wonderful encounter—"

"How did you know?" he asked quickly.

"The open door," she replied, pointing over her shoulder. "Boss, you've got to see that as long as the grudge is
there, you will always run the risk of that happening." She
peered up at him, her face etched with a combination of
worry and determination. "You can't love the way you
need to love when there's anger in your heart."

He didn't know what to say, how to respond. Next to
his mother, he'd had more deep conversations with
Regina than any other person in his life. She always
listened, truly listened, when he needed to talk. She

knew the things that hurt him deeply. She'd offered opinions in the past, stood beside him through it all. But never, until now, had she seemed to take his father's side. Tate stiffened.

"I'm not saying your hurt and anger aren't justified. Please know that." She stood up and leaned against the desk alongside him. "I'm just saying that as long as you carry those things in your heart…as long as you fail to make some sort of peace with the past…you can't truly enjoy the present and the future."

Her words filtered through his mind, causing a tug in his heart. Was she right? Was he allowing incidents in his past to sabotage today?

"I think your mom would tell you the very same thing if she were here," Regina murmured. "If I didn't believe that I would never have risked my job the way I just did."

A stinging he recognized all too well began in the back of his eyes, threatening to work its way forward in a show of emotion he'd prefer to bypass. "Regina, not a day has gone by since you started here that I haven't valued your input. Today hasn't changed that. But the stuff with my dad…I just *can't*."

She started toward the door, stopping midway. "Maybe you can't. Maybe you won't. Just remember, the stuff with your dad isn't the only grudge you harbor."

"Meaning?"

"Meaning Phoebe lives on Quinton Lane, right?"

He nodded, unsure of where Regina was going.

"Well, then, you've also got to get past your grudge toward Phoebe's neighbors."

"They were wrong, Regina."

She crossed to the door, placing her hand on the knob before turning to meet his eyes once again. "I know. And I'm not telling you to apologize. I'm simply saying that maybe it's time to *show* them they were wrong about you."

Chapter Eight

Phoebe switched on the small rectangular monitor and sank onto the couch, her body aching in places she didn't know had muscles. The pain in her lower back was compliments of Mrs. Applewhite's old pine chest, the heaviness in her thighs a reminder of all the steps she'd climbed with assorted pieces of furniture. The stiffness in her shoulders was no doubt a result of reaching into Ms. Weatherby's attic for one box of books after another—twenty-five in all.

The work had been tedious and exhausting, with limited physical help from her elderly neighbors. Yet those who were unable to hoist boxes and sort through years of accumulated stuff had been godsends in keeping Kayla busy so Phoebe could keep things moving.

Monday afternoon had disappeared in a blur, with the same activities forecasted for Tuesday, Wednesday and Thursday. Friday would be for pricing and setup, with all their efforts coming to what they hoped would be a profitable culmination on Saturday morning.

If she could even get out of bed by then.

Phoebe stretched her right arm across her chest and

massaged her left shoulder, wincing at the soreness, which had grown worse throughout the day. It was at times like these, when evening had descended and the day's work was done, that she was most aware of Gram's absence. The realization hit anew every night, as if her grandmother's passing had taken place days rather than years earlier.

Phoebe suspected part of tonight's sadness spawned from her constant contact with people her grandmother would have loved. The rest probably tied to the heightened sense of loneliness that had been hovering since her visit to Tate's office.

She'd felt so alive in his arms, so keenly aware of the powerful physical connection they shared. And it hadn't been just her. She knew that. His yearning as he'd kissed her had been undeniable.

There was no doubt about it. Tate's lips on hers had revived something inside her she'd thought was gone for good. His tenderness as he'd pulled her toward him was nothing short of intoxicating. And she longed to experience that feeling again.

With him.

Unfortunately, the man who had kissed her was a far cry from the man who'd railed at her not once, but twice, *and* frightened Kayla.

That Doug's unyielding nature had ended their relationship with such finality wasn't really a surprise. He'd shown signs of it in virtually everything he did. She'd just been too young and naive to recognize it.

But with Tate there had been nothing during their time together on Saturday to suggest his inability, or his *unwillingness,* to be open-minded. Not many men would have deliberately crossed enemy lines just to offer an apology for something that wasn't entirely their fault. Not many men would've been so willing to share a deep-rooted hurt with a woman they barely knew. Not many men would listen to a woman's sad story with the genuine concern Tate had shown. And not many men could kiss like he kissed....

"Good grief." Determined to get Tate and his knee-weakening kisses out of her mind, she reached for one of her art magazines and flipped it open, thumbing through the pages with little to no interest, her heart aching all the while for an opportunity to talk through her feelings with her grandmother.

Sure, she could speak to Mrs. Haskell or Ms. Weatherby, but it wasn't the same. Family was different, special.

Why couldn't Tate see that?

Tossing the magazine back where she'd found it, Phoebe swung her legs onto the sofa and snuggled her head against the armrest. As much as it hurt, she had to admit, Tate Williams wanted nothing more to do with her. His failure to call or stop by since the incident at his office was all the proof she needed. She wasn't happy about that, but it was what it was as her grandmother always said.

But just because he wanted nothing to do with *her* didn't mean Phoebe couldn't make an attempt at playing fairy godmother where he and his dad were concerned. Maybe they were destined to be at odds. Maybe nothing could fix their rift. But they wouldn't know if they didn't try.

They just needed a little shove. And shove she would—one way or another.

Phoebe turned her head and squinted through the darkness toward the fireplace on the other side of the room. She didn't need a lamp to see the pictures scattered across the mantel. She'd memorized every feature, the details of each and every face. There was the picture with her parents before they'd perished in a car accident the morning of her first birthday. There was the snapshot from her first day of kindergarten with Gram beaming in the background. The photo of her and Gram at Phoebe's graduation from college, and the one of Kayla in her arms shortly after delivery. But it was the picture on the far right that made her sit up straight.

Her grandparents had been sweethearts since the second grade and had remained so until the day he died. And although he'd passed on before Phoebe was born, he'd come alive in her mind through Gram's stories and memories.

Listening to Bart recount his feelings for Lorraine and Mary had struck a chord in Phoebe. The regret he'd described over wasting time with Mary had resonated deep inside her soul, as had the cruel way in which his love for Lorraine had been ripped from his hands.

Phoebe wished with all her might that Bart could have just one more day with Mary, to tell her all the things he should have said while she was still alive.

Her death made that impossible.

But maybe it wasn't too late to make things right with Lorraine. To explain what had happened and why. To make peace with something that had such a profound impact on his life.

Without really realizing what she was doing, Phoebe rose from the couch and moved toward the small alcove off the kitchen. She knew the chance of finding anything about Lorraine Walters was slim to none, but if there was even the remotest possibility it would come from the Internet.

Bending slowly so as to minimize the discomfort in her back, Phoebe turned on her desktop and waited while it booted up. Once the final screen was ready, Phoebe sat down on the small cushioned chair and began searching for any information she could find on Bart's first love.

It was easy to rule out the first three hits based on age, with the subject being either a little too old or a little too young. The fourth was an obituary notice.

Holding her breath, she clicked on the name and began reading, hoping against hope it wasn't Bart's Lorraine. Fortunately, mention of the woman's educational background erased any possible connection between the two.

The fifth and final hit brought a tingle down her spine.

Lorraine Walters-Finney of Groverton, Ohio, was recognized by city officials for her tireless efforts to raise funds for a veteran's memorial in Groverton Park. When asked why the cause was so near and dear to her heart, Walters-Finney declined to comment beyond saying, "We've all been touched by a veteran in one way or another."

Phoebe scrolled through the rest of the article, noting geographical similarities between Bart Williams and the Lorraine Walters featured on the screen in front of her. The final confirmation came near the bottom, when the reporter mentioned the woman's lifelong interest in knitting.

"Bingo." Her heart pounding, Phoebe pulled the bottom phone book from under a pile of directories she kept in the corner and flipped it open. Although Groverton was an hour or so from Cedarville, it had been in the same coverage area as the home where she'd lived with Gram.

In her haste, she passed by the correct page several times before finding the entry she was seeking: LW Finney. 14 Sunbeam Lane. Groverton. 513-555-3324.

Glancing at the clock on the bottom of the computer screen, she reached for the phone and began to dial.

TATE WALKED FROM room to room, unable to sit still long enough to start on his next design or to even watch a little mindless television. He'd been restless ever since he got home, Regina's words endlessly nagging at his thoughts and emotions.

After a fourth or fifth lap around the first floor, Tate finally chose his refuge—the kitchen.

When he'd been a boy, the kitchen was always the go-to place when he'd had trouble at school with a classmate or difficulty on an English test. A few words of encouragement from his mom over a freshly baked chocolate chip cookie and a tall glass of cold milk had always made problems disappear. Or at the very least, seem manageable.

But even as he crossed the threshold into his own kitchen, he knew it wasn't the location that had provided the comfort and the healing. It had been the person inside. His mother.

That was why his minimansion hadn't felt like a true home since day one. Sure, the ooh-aah factor was obvious around every corner. The massive stone fireplaces and floor-to-ceiling windows off the back of the home drew that reaction all on their own. But it was *warmth* that was sorely lacking.

He'd certainly tried to convey a welcoming feeling when he'd designed the place, and from an architectural standpoint, he had succeeded. The kitchen itself was a masterpiece, with every modern convenience in just the perfect spot to create edible works of art. An incredible feature for anyone with a talent or interest in cooking.

Of which he had neither.

With a gentle tug on the fingerprint-free, stainless-steel handle, he stepped back and surveyed the contents of his freezer. Pizza in various sizes and shapes, an assortment of TV dinners and a few tubs of ice cream reflected the extent of his culinary aspirations. If it couldn't be microwaved or scooped into a bowl, he didn't make it. That's what take-out menus, client dinners and close-knit families were for.

Or two out of three, in his case.

He pushed the door shut, his hands empty. Despite the late hour, he simply wasn't in the mood to eat. The three-hour lunch with his soon-to-be partners probably had something to do with that. So, too, did Regina's comments. But the pièce de résistance was his atrocious behavior toward Phoebe.

Leaning against a bar stool, Tate thought back to the conversation with his secretary.

"You can't love the way you need to love when there's anger in your heart."

It made sense. All he needed to do was look back at his own mother to realize there was some validity to Regina's words. It didn't take a rocket scientist to see his parents' marriage had been anything but perfect. His mother had been head over heels in love with Tate's father, who in turn had been tolerant at best. But somehow, his mom had remained happy. Not a grin-and-bear-it kind, but a true inner joy that had radiated from every ounce of her being. The kind of sincere happiness that transformed the tiny little kitchen on Quinton Lane into a kid's safe harbor. Day after day. Cookies or no cookies.

By contrast, *he* was the one who'd grown bitter watching his mom give and give and give, his father taking it all for granted with no detectable appreciation for any of it.

They were memories he recalled often. And what did he have in his life to show for the anger and the bitterness? A great big expensive home that had been decorated with the kind of professional flair one might find in a museum—all class, no warmth. And as for a relationship? Nada. Zip.

Tate drummed his fingers on the countertop and looked around the room. Sure, he had solid cherry cabinetry, stainless-steel appliances, copper pots hanging over the cook's island and slate floors. It was the best designed and equipped kitchen money could buy. Yet, if he was honest with himself, he felt more at home in Phoebe's cramped kitchen than he ever had here. And he suspected it had very little to do with his own memories of the place and a lot to do with her sweet personality and natural warmth. Things he couldn't recreate on a piece of draft paper no matter how hard he tried.

Phoebe.

It drove him absolutely nuts to think back on the

way he'd yelled at her for something as innocent as an invitation to spend an afternoon together, all but belittling her for what was just well-meaning, albeit misguided, sentiment. His sour relationship with his father wasn't her fault or even something she could've known about. And Kayla? Tate had been a giant-size jerk scaring such a sweet, happy-go-lucky baby.

Growling at himself, he left the stool and walked to the French doors that led to his professionally landscaped patio and flower garden—simplicities of life he'd hired someone else to plant and nurture. He unlocked the handle and stepped out into the darkness, relishing the stars twinkling overhead and the absolute quiet of the night. It had been an adjustment to fall asleep to silence after growing up on Quinton Lane with the sounds of older cars heading to and from jobs at all hours.

While he couldn't imagine forgiving his dad, Tate *could* step back and try to see the Quinton Lane mess from his neighbors' point of view. He himself had been guilty of making assumptions about Phoebe. He'd assumed the nature of her career based on exterior things like clothes and a car. Just as his neighbors had made false assumptions about him based on a level of education and the address of his employer.

And if he allowed himself to be objective, Tate could understand why they'd come to the conclusions they did. He'd been the first kid on Quinton Lane ever to go to college. That alone made him different. Throw in the white-collar job, the ignorance of a corporate pecking order, and all of a sudden their inability to comprehend what he could and couldn't do was easier to swallow. Or at least ponder with an open mind.

Moving to West Cedarville to lick his wounds had simply been the final nail in the coffin as far as the neighbors were concerned. The young boy they'd loved and supported was suddenly too good for them.

It wasn't true. Not by a long shot.

He plopped down on a chaise longue and stared up at the quarter moon, its limited light casting shadows across the ground. If Mrs. Applewhite and Mr. Borden and the rest of the crew had only known how much it hurt him to be powerless against the city, to be unable to keep them from taking over Les Walker's property so long ago…

Sighing, he laced his fingers behind his head and imagined the fight he'd have given if he'd had the kind of power and reputation he had now.

"That's it!" He sat up, his feet hitting the patio with a thud. In an instant he was back inside and heading for the rear staircase off the kitchen.

"It's time to show them they were wrong about you."

For the first time all day, Regina's words brought a smile to Tate's lips and hope to his heart. He may have been a little fish in a big pond at one time, but no more. Taking the steps two at a time, he reached the top landing and headed in the direction of his den. There was no doubt he wanted to show the Quinton Laners they'd been wrong about him. Because they were. Big-time.

But even more than that, he wanted to show Phoebe who he was—inside and out. Prove to her he wasn't the kind of guy who made a habit out of yelling at women and scaring innocent babies.

Chapter Nine

Phoebe could feel her muscles beginning to relax as she propped her head on her hand and stretched out across the rug. The Haskells' home had been the easiest to cull thus far, thanks to the extra pair of capable arms belonging to their thirty-three-year-old son, John. Still, three days in a row of constant bending, lifting and carrying had taken its toll on her energy level, making floor play seem like heaven at the moment.

"Dis?"

"That's a spatula."

Kayla's tiny hand disappeared inside the navy blue mixing bowl long enough to extract another item, poking her fingers through the center holes before setting it on the top of her head.

"Dis?"

Phoebe laughed and shook her head. "That's not a hat, silly. It's a slotted spoon."

"Ooon."

"Good girl!" Phoebe's praise was followed by the sudden rustle of Kayla's overalls as she took off across the living room.

Boots.

Sure enough, the orange-and-white fur ball who had spent the majority of the day napping in a sunny spot, had made the mistake of walking past Kayla en route to his food bowl. In an instant the fascinating world of kitchen utensils took a backseat to the thrill of an afternoon chase, with Kayla gaining ground on the still-groggy cat.

Grateful for the momentary reprieve, Phoebe flipped onto her back and stared up at the ceiling. The day's prep work for the tag sale had been shorter than she'd expected, allowing Kayla to nap in her own crib and Phoebe to grab a much-needed shower. The massage setting on the showerhead had worked wonders on her sore back and shoulders, giving her a boost until she could collapse into bed, only to get up and do it all over again tomorrow.

Phoebe glanced at the clock on the mantel and groaned softly. If it weren't for Kayla, she'd ditch dinner in favor of vegging on the couch for a few hours. But she couldn't and she knew it. Skipping meals wasn't an option when you had a baby, not a healthy one, anyway. Still, Phoebe actually found herself imagining a benefit of Doug's wealthy lifestyle: having food prepared and waiting at the table each and every night.

But as quickly as the image came, it disappeared, replaced by memories of cooking side-by-side with Gram, experimenting with this ingredient or that sauce. *That* was what she wanted for Kayla. Not cooks and servants catering to her every whim.

She sat up and looked around, the corners of her mouth lifting at the sight of the denim-clad bottom disappearing around the corner, lap two of the Kayla-Boots 500 well under way.

"Okay, break it up, you two. It's time for—"

A soft knock cut her sentence short, replacing it with a sense of dread in the pit of her stomach. She adored her neighbors, she really did. She just needed a little time to regroup before enduring another day of ailment stories and city-official bashing.

Sighing, Phoebe turned the corner into the front entryway, looking back over her shoulder to gauge Kayla's whereabouts. Lap three was almost complete, with a beleaguered Boots still claiming the lead. For now.

"Hang in there, Boots, only another ten or so laps to go," she said, her laughter coming to a halt at the sight of the man standing outside her door.

Tate.

She swallowed as he smiled at her and lifted his hand in a wave. Sure, there was a part of her that wanted to see him again, but his open hostility toward her the last two times they'd spoken was tough to ignore.

Unlocking the dead bolt, Phoebe pulled the door open, her body firmly planted between him and her home. "Hi."

His index finger shot into the air before he disappeared around the corner, returning seconds later with a bouquet of roses in his hand. "I'm sorry I was such an idiot the other day. I had no right to blow up at you for what was nothing more than a thoughtful invitation." He held out the flowers, his sheepish grin breaking down her willpower. "And I'm doubly sorry for reacting so harshly to your efforts yesterday morning."

"I—I don't know what to say." She took the roses

from his outstretched hand, her own beginning to shake as she pulled them toward her nose and breathed in their scent. "You didn't need to bring me flowers."

"I wanted to." His gaze moved past her, focused on Kayla as she broke from the racecourse to head in their direction. "I have something for you, too, Kayla."

Startled, Phoebe turned in time to see Tate disappear around the corner for a few more seconds, reappearing this time with a tiny white teddy bear in his hand. He set it on the ground beside Phoebe's feet and waited for Kayla to approach it on her own.

"Phoebe, I am so sorry for the way I reacted. For being so rude to you and for scaring Kayla half to death. I don't know what came over me."

She blinked against the unexpected tears that threatened to make them both uncomfortable and fixed her gaze instead on Kayla. The baby had stopped next to her to cuddle the stuffed bear.

"Phoebe?" Tate murmured.

She glanced up, her eyes stinging as she met his, the apprehension on his face as tangible as the roses in her hand and the bear in Kayla's arms. "Tate…I didn't mean to cause a problem by inviting you to go with us that day. And I wasn't trying to cause you pain by saying that about your dad. I was just—" She closed her eyes briefly and inhaled slowly, willing her voice to steadiness before she made a complete fool of herself. "I was just trying to help."

He took hold of her hand and squeezed it gently. "I know. I realize that, I really do. It's just that I'm not… I mean, my father and I aren't close. We haven't been since my mother died. Or really *ever,* for that matter. She was the glue that held us together." He stroked the top of Phoebe's hand with his thumb, his eyes locked with hers. "But regardless of my issues, you didn't deserve those ridiculous outbursts. I wasn't angry at you. I really wasn't."

Her skin tingled at the sensation of his hand on hers, a feeling rivaled only by the memory of being in his arms…

"Have you eaten yet?" he asked.

Before she could absorb his question, he disappeared around the corner once again, this time returning with a large picnic basket in one hand and a folded blanket in the other.

She felt her heart rate accelerate as she stared at him as his words took root in her mind. "I, um, don't understand. What is that?"

He laughed. "It's dinner. Yours, Kayla's and mine. If you'll give me a second chance at being a nice guy."

"Wow." It was all she could think to say at the moment, a simple word that summed up her feelings.

"C'mon. I know the perfect spot." He cast his eyes downward, a grin exploding across his face. "I'll carry the basket and blanket if you'll bring Kayla and her bear."

"But the flowers…" She tightened her grasp on the bouquet. "I need to put them in water."

"Bring them. They'll make a great centerpiece for our blanket."

For a moment she thought she was dreaming. A gorgeous guy was standing on her front step, all but begging her to accompany him on a picnic. Her *and* *Kayla*. But if she was truly dreaming, she wouldn't be wearing a pair of ratty gray shorts and a white ribbed cami, her hair still damp from the shower.

"Please?"

If nothing else, Tate Williams was a man who wasn't afraid to apologize. She just wished he could do it in a way that wouldn't threaten to sweep her off her feet.

It's just dinner. Give the poor guy a break.

"Okay." Juggling the bouquet, she reached down, lifted Kayla into her arms and stepped outside, pulling the door shut behind them. "Where are we going?"

"Not far. And fortunately for you, you're quite a bit smaller than I am so my body should act as a great shield for you and Kayla."

She stepped off her front porch and turned to look at Tate. "Shield? For what?"

"Apples, oranges, gunshots…that sort of thing." He fell into step beside her, his words giving way to a small laugh as she stopped walking and looked at him.

"You lost me somewhere between the apples and the bullets."

"I was being funny," he said, wedging the blanket under his elbow so he could brush a strand of hair from her cheek, his touch causing her body to tingle in places that probably shouldn't be tingling with her daughter in her arms. "Besides, I don't think Mrs. Applewhite believes in throwing *fruit.*"

Ahh, now she understood.

"And the bullets?" she asked, a teasing lilt to her voice as they resumed their walk once again.

"Fruit's one thing. Bullets, I fear, are an entirely different matter."

It had been a long time since she'd felt as young and carefree as she did at that moment, her fear of being hurt dissipating long enough to enable her to enjoy a nice evening with someone her own age.

Phoebe stole a glance in Tate's direction, her face reddening as their eyes met.

"I'm willing to take my chances with the bullets." She knew her voice was unnaturally quiet, even a little shaky, but she hoped he heard her words.

The warmth of Tate's touch on the small of her back made her breath hitch ever so slightly. "That, Phoebe Jennings, is *exactly* what I was hoping you'd say."

HE TRIED TO FOCUS on the contents of the basket, but it was damn near impossible with a woman like Phoebe Jennings within arm's reach. Her hair spilled over her shoulders in soft waves while a few stray tendrils curled around her ears, framing her heart-shaped face. She sat near him on the blanket, her long, smooth legs taunting him. Her lips were parted ever so slightly, making his own ache to taste hers once again.

"So what do you have in there?" Phoebe straightened her back and peeked over the side of the basket, the lowering sun lighting up her greenish-brown eyes.

He dropped the lid shut and shook his head mockingly. "All good things come to those who wait. Didn't anyone ever teach you that, Miss Jennings?"

"As a matter of fact, yes. My grandmother did." Phoebe glanced sideways in Kayla's direction before looking back at him with a mischievous twinkle in her eye. "However, *Mr. Williams,* a longer and more relaxed picnic comes to those who feed the baby before she gets cranky. Did anyone ever tell you *that?*"

He looked over at the baby happily picking clover in the middle of the grassy field. It was hard to imagine such a happy kid getting cranky.

"Nope. Haven't learned that lesson yet. But I'm looking forward to the class." Tate opened the basket once again, removing a small container. "I did a search online this afternoon and macaroni and cheese got the most rave reports from moms for kids Kayla's age. Something about the noodles being easy to pick up."

He set the container down on the blanket, along with a brand-new baby bib. Reaching into the basket once more, he extracted a sippy cup with kittens on the outside and apple juice on the inside. "And this should fill the fruit quota, though if you want her to have more, I brought a jar of pears just in case."

Phoebe's sharp inhalation made him glance upward, his mind racing to figure out what he'd forgotten.

Main course, fruit, dessert...

"Oh. I got her a treat, too. I just figured I shouldn't show her that yet. Macaroni and cheese, although good, is no match for a chocolate chip cookie."

"No. It's not that." Phoebe's voice softened to a near whisper as she looked out into the distance, the sun's rays revealing the sudden glistening in her eyes. "I just can't believe you went to all this effort to apologize."

It took everything he had not to pull her to him, to cradle her in his arms, to feel her body against his. But he'd promised himself he'd take it slow, give her time to trust.

Instead, he reached out, traced her jawline with his thumb. "The apology got me to your door. This—" he removed his hand from her face to gesture to the picnic items set out on the blanket "—is about wanting to spend time with you. And Kayla, too."

He rubbed a tendril of Phoebe's hair between his fingers before dropping his hand to his side. He wanted those beautiful eyes turned on him, the sparkle he'd detected earlier back where it belonged. And he was determined to make it happen.

"Now, before you think I've forgotten *you,* let's see what else is in here, shall we?"

She nibbled her lower lip and his body tightened in response. Never in his life had he come across a woman who could convey such strength and vulnerability at the same time. It intrigued him in both a physical and an emotional way.

"Okay. I give up. What *do* you have in there for us?" She leaned forward, the crest of her rounded breasts visible over the top of her white cami. "Something yummy, I hope."

Tate swallowed quickly, wrestling with his body's urge to take her right there on the blanket. "Uh, what?"

Her laughter echoed across the empty field, making him shift on the blanket in a desperate attempt to get comfortable. "I asked if you had anything yummy in there for us."

"Oh." Clearing his throat, he dug back into the basket and removed four wrapped packages. "I didn't know what you liked best, so I got a few different sandwich meats—turkey, ham, roast beef and chicken." He set them on the blanket. "I have a couple different cheeses in this package and just about every topping you might want in here."

She smiled, the sparkle in her eyes returning in spades. "You are amazing, Tate Williams. You thought of everything."

"Wait. Not yet, there's more." He reached into the basket one last time, pulling two wine goblets and a covered plate from the bottom. "It wouldn't be much of a picnic without some wine and chocolate-covered strawberries."

As he set down the last item, he looked up and smiled. "I'm glad you agreed to give me a shot."

"How could I not? No one has ever shown up on my doorstep with a picnic basket before."

"Good." He watched as Phoebe stood up and walked over to where Kayla was clearing the earth of all things white and fluffy. Lifting her daughter in her arms, she returned to the blanket, the gentle sway of her hips hypnotizing.

Setting the baby down, Phoebe sat beside her, snapping open the macaroni and cheese container with a practiced hand. "This looks really good. Did you make it yourself?"

"Nah. Maggie did. I told her what I needed and she whipped up a batch while she was at the house."

Phoebe secured the bib around Kayla's neck. "Who's Maggie?"

"My housekeeper. Generally, she doesn't cook, as I prefer to just do my own thing in the evenings. But I asked if she could help out this one time so I wouldn't end up getting to your house at ten o'clock."

At the mention of his housekeeper he felt a shift in Phoebe's mood. Nothing he could put his finger on exactly; it was just a feeling. A sense. He debated calling her on it, but opted to let it go. There would be time for that kind of exploration in the future. If he didn't blow it today.

"Hey, any luck on an idea for this place?" He waved his hand to indicate the green space between the Haskells and the Weatherbys.

"Not yet. I'm just hoping we make enough money at Saturday's tag sale to buy a few trees. Maybe if we do things to enhance the environment the city will leave us alone."

Doubtful, he knew, but Tate chose to let that go unsaid for the moment, too. Besides, he had a plan that just might fly with the city. A plan he'd rather keep to himself until he worked everything out—on paper and with city officials.

Instead, he asked her about her childhood and her family. As she talked, he couldn't help but notice the way her voice grew more and more animated when she spoke of her grandmother, growing quiet again when she shared the ache she still felt at the woman's loss.

From there, conversation moved from topic to topic, their dinner disappearing along with the last remnants of the sun. When the sandwiches and side salads were finally gone he uncovered the plate of strawberries and offered one to Phoebe. She grinned and reached for a small one in the center.

"Thank you so much for tonight, Tate. I think I needed a little companionship more than I realized. And the food was delicious."

"I'm glad you enjoyed it." He offered her more wine, adding a swallow or two to his own glass when she declined. Slowly, he swirled the liquid around the bottom of his goblet, pondering a fact he simply couldn't ignore.

He wasn't ready for the evening to end. He was enjoying Phoebe's company too much.

"I think Kayla had fun, too." Phoebe raised a finger to her lips, then pointed toward the edge of the blanket. "She's out like a light."

Tate felt the corners of his mouth tug upward at the sight of the sleeping baby. Then Phoebe's lips recaptured his attention.

Carefully, he set his glass down on top of the closed basket and leaned forward, cupping the back of her head with his hand. He eased toward her, his core temperature rising as the tip of her tongue slid across her top lip. That one innocent response was more than he could take and he pulled her toward him hungrily, his mouth closing on hers, his tongue penetrating in heated exploration.

He felt her palm slip down his chest to the bottom of his shirt then reach around to his back, where her nails dug gently into his skin, pulling him closer. His heart began to pound as their kiss intensified, his skin burning at her touch, the bulge in his pants becoming almost unbearable.

Slow it down, buddy. Slow it down.

Mustering every ounce of willpower he could find, he pulled back with a soft growl. "You are amazing, Phoebe."

The tinge of pink that sprang to her cheeks made him want her all the more, but he resisted. Next time, when they were alone, he'd take it further. All the way if she'd let him.

"You are, too, Tate." Her words were soft, raspy even, as she began gathering the trash into a small pile.

He reached down, grasped her warm fingers in his. "My firm is having a reception on Saturday night. At the Autumn Room in West Cedarville. I'd love for you to come with me."

"The Autumn Room?" A look he couldn't identify passed across her face as she gently removed her hand from his and continued collecting the wrappings and containers. "Isn't that a really nice place?"

"Uh-huh." He popped another strawberry into his mouth and tucked the plate into the basket. "Five-star."

"Well, I don't know. We have the tag sale that day and—"

"That's in the morning, right?" he prompted.

Her face reddened slightly. "Yeah. I guess. And I've got Kayla too."

"Bring her."

She stopped and stared at him. "She's a wonderful baby, Tate, but the Autumn Room? That's no place for a child, nor is a company function."

Confused, he leaned across the blanket and took both her hands in his. "What's wrong, Phoebe? Tonight was great, wasn't it?"

Her eyes closed momentarily, but she opened them again and managed a wan smile. "You're right. I'll find someone to sit Kayla. I'd love to be your guest."

"Good. I'll pick you up at seven." He released her right hand so he could touch her face, guide her gaze upward to meet his. "We'll have a good time. I guarantee it."

Her smile spread ever so slightly, her lips seeming to tremble. Had he done something wrong? Everything had been going so well—

"What do I wear?"

The question surprised him and he studied her, noted the look of uncertainty in her eyes. "Whatever you want. You'll be beautiful no matter what."

She slowly nodded. "Okay. I'll do my best."

Chapter Ten

After a relatively slow start, the Quinton Lane tag sale was the place to be that Saturday morning. Car after car delivered eager shoppers intent on finding great bargains. The fact that Quinton Lane was known throughout Cedarville proper as a long-standing staple of the community, thanks to that generation's pride in their hard-earned possessions, certainly helped.

A young family from six roads over had hit the biggest jackpot so far that morning, securing a four-piece oak bedroom set for a hundred bucks. They'd been blown away by the condition of the furniture, while Eunice Weatherby had been pleased to know her late son's furniture would be a part of the formative years of yet another child.

Phoebe plopped Kayla into the play station she'd set up beside Mr. Borden's table, then busied herself counting out change for one of his customers while he engaged in an intense negotiation over his boyhood train set. She chuckled to herself, listening to the teenager raising his offer fifty cents at a time until he reached the original asking price.

"Sheesh, he drives a hard bargain." The youth reached into the back pocket of his jeans and extracted a twenty-dollar bill. "I tried to get him to come down to ten and he wouldn't budge. *At all.*"

Phoebe took the money from the boy's outstretched hand and placed it in the metal cash box. "Mr. Borden was a professional livestock auctioneer when he was a young man. You didn't stand a chance. Really."

The teenager laughed. "You mean I was had?"

At her nod, he shrugged. "Ahhh, that's okay. I still did pretty good. And it's going to be cool talking trains with him now."

Leave it to Mr. Borden to make a friend at the drop of a hat. There was something about the man that attracted people to him regardless of their age. "If you get to spend time with him because of that sale, then *you're* the one coming out ahead."

The boy grabbed the box with the train set and grinned. "Yeah, I kinda sensed that. He reminds me of my grandpa out in California."

"I know what you mean." Phoebe thanked the boy for his purchase, then watched as he stopped to shake the elderly man's hand one last time before mounting the black ten-speed leaning against a nearby tree.

After glancing at her wristwatch, she squatted down next to Kayla and smoothed a lock of baby-fine hair from her forehead. "You're being a very good little helper this morning. And we're almost done." She kissed her daughter's chubby cheek before retrieving a set of stacking blocks that had slipped out of her reach. "Here you go, sweetie."

Phoebe straightened up and made her way over to

Mr. Borden, who was accepting a crisp fifty-dollar bill from a woman in exchange for a set of pristine golf clubs. Her neighbor's erect posture and face-splitting smile was proof positive he was enjoying the tag sale.

And he wasn't the only one. Eunice Weatherby had taken great delight in sharing tried-and-true parenting tips with each and every person of childbearing age who stopped at her table. The Haskells had sold all of their son's old sporting equipment within an hour of the sale's start, and Mrs. Applewhite had been in her element, running her table with an iron fist.

"Well, Phoebe, I haven't had this much fun in a long time." Mr. Borden gave her hand a squeeze before grasping the top bars of his walker and heading in the direction of the table. "I don't know how the others did, but I think my stuff brought in a few hundred dollars. Everyone seemed to enjoy what I was selling. Though—" he looked both ways with a mischievous gleam in his eyes "—that young man who wanted my train set was my favorite customer by far."

Phoebe laughed. "You taught him a thing or two, that's for sure."

"Darn tootin'." Mr. Borden removed the top tray from the cash box and sat down in the lone folding chair, his hands scooping out money. "I'll count this and keep an eye on your little princess here if you'll snoop around and find out what everyone else made."

"Everyone?"

His face reddened slightly. "Some more than others, I guess."

"You mean *one* more than others, don't you?"

He grimaced. "Okay—yeah. I'm curious about

everyone, but mostly Gertrude." He paused for a moment to clear his throat. "Not that it's a competition or anything."

"Of course it's not. It's not like you take great pride in beating Mrs. Applewhite every chance you get," Phoebe teased.

"Do I do that?" he asked innocently.

"I see you pushing your walker a bit faster whenever you two are walking side by side. I see you adding fake flowers among your real ones to get more color in the spring, and I know you added an extra bag of chocolate chips to those cookies you brought to the last potluck."

He coughed, sat quietly, then coughed again. "You caught me. But Phoebe, she makes it fun. She lives to win and tell everyone about it. You know that."

It was true.

Shaking her head, Phoebe kissed the top of his head and then waved at Kayla. "I'll be right back, sweetie. I have some spying to do real quick."

"I knew you were a good girl, Phoebe Jennings."

"I think the more appropriate word would be *corrupt*." She winked at her favorite neighbor, then went to find the answers he sought.

It didn't take long to get a total from the rest of her neighbors, since each one had already begun counting. Ms. Weatherby's furniture collection, clothes and kitchen supplies drew just over a hundred fifty dollars. Mrs. Applewhite's knickknacks, decades-long book collection and furniture netted two hundred and forty-five dollars. The Haskells came in at two hundred and fifteen with everything from sporting goods and toys, to tools and assorted bits of furniture. Other neighbors who'd gotten into the act had raised a nice chunk, as well.

Armed with a tiny slip of paper she'd commandeered from the Jorgans' table, Phoebe returned to her starting point. "Okay. The one to beat is Mrs. Applewhite."

Mr. Borden looked up, squinting in concentration. "How much?"

"I don't know if I should tell you." Phoebe tucked the paper behind her back with what she hoped was her most angelic expression. "I mean, I don't want you to feel bad if you fell short of her take."

"Fell short?" Mr. Borden exhaled loudly through pursed lips, his wrinkled hand tapping the table in a familiar rhythm.

"That's not… Is that—"

"It most certainly is," he crowed. "And I'm tapping it because I'm quite confident my table was the day's cash cow."

"Ehhh." Kayla's hands shot up into the air, her feet running in place beneath the play tray.

"See?" He pointed at the baby. "Even *she* wants to know how much I won by."

Phoebe rolled her eyes in mock disgust and reached for her daughter. "Actually, I think she just wants some lunch. It's been a long day."

The elderly man rummaged through the tote bag beside his chair and extracted a package of crackers. He un- wrapped the plastic covering and set one into Kayla's eager hands before looking back at Phoebe. *"How much?"*

"Two hundred forty-five."

"Hah!" Mr. Borden grabbed hold of his walker and pulled himself to his feet, his backside dancing around as he put lyrics to the music he'd been tapping. "'We're in the money, We're in the money'… I beat 'em all…yesss, I did."

Kayla's hands, covered in wet cracker crumbs, began clapping along to a beat all her own, her squeals of delight filling the gaps between Mr. Borden's lyrics.

"I take it you did better?" Phoebe grinned at her before looking back at Mr. Borden.

"Two hundred and fifty-two!"

"*Seven bucks?* That's all?" Phoebe asked, her lips twitching.

"I beat her, didn't I? That makes those seven bucks worth far, *far* more." Mr. Borden winked at her as he lowered himself back onto his chair and patted the table beside him. "Well, now that we've got *that* squared away, sit. Tell me what's got you so quiet this morning."

Phoebe looked at him questioningly. "I'm not quiet. I've just been busy, that's all."

The man shook his head slowly and leaned back against the chair. "I know busy and I know quiet. And while you've certainly been the former, you've also been the latter."

Glancing down at her folded hands, Phoebe shrugged.

"Does it have to do with your new fellow?"

Her head snapped up; her cheeks warmed. "Fellow?"

"Tate Williams."

She considered feigning ignorance for all of about two seconds, but knew it was futile. Somehow, news of Tate's impromptu picnic had made its way through the Quinton Lane pipeline.

"Now I'm not grilling you. Please know that. Truth be told, I'm glad someone's finally woken up and realized what a gem you are."

Her face grew warmer.

"But there's an uncertainty about you today that I can't help but notice. And I'm here if you want to talk. You're like a granddaughter to me, Phoebe. You know that."

And she did.

"You're okay with that *someone* being the infamous Tate Williams?" Her voice was barely audible, causing Mr. Borden to lean forward and mess with the hearing aid behind his right ear.

She repeated her question.

"Tate Williams was always a good boy. A very good boy. That whole mess about the city council and Les Walker's house got blown way out of proportion."

"You realize that?"

"Of course I do. Sure, there was a time I wasn't so certain. Didn't understand the way things are done in the professional world." He traced a finger along the top bar of his walker. "I auctioned off pigs, for gosh sake. But Bart set us all straight. At least those of us who would listen, anyway."

"And Mrs. Applewhite?"

A frustrated sign emerged from Mr. Borden's chest. "She was one who wouldn't listen. You think she's competitive *now?* You should have seen her back when Tate was a young boy. Mary Williams was a thorn in Gertrude's side because we all adored her. Drove the woman batty." He paused to consider his words. "Who knows, maybe that's why she's so…well, you know. Anyway, I don't think she lost much sleep when we all started questioning Tate back then."

"And now? Why does everyone stand by and let her keep going with this?" Phoebe asked.

"I guess we're all afraid to cross her for fear she'll keel over from the stress. You know how she gets. The way she complains about pains in her chest."

Phoebe heard his words, absorbed them, but then drew up short when something he'd said earlier finally registered. "Did you say *Bart* went to bat for Tate?"

"I did." Mr. Borden shifted in his seat, another grimace flashing across his face. "He gave us a dressing-down after Mary's funeral on account of the cold shoulder Tate received."

"He was treated badly at his mother's funeral?" She knew her tone was shrill, even a little angry, but she couldn't help it. Tate's lingering hurt made all the more sense now.

Her neighbor dropped his head briefly, in silent agreement.

"Then why didn't you say something last week, when she was yelling at him in the street after our meeting?" Phoebe asked.

"Most of us were gone, if you'll remember. I heard the ruckus as I was walking home, but couldn't hear or see well enough to know what was going on."

She stood beside the table, mulling over everything she'd just heard, her heart aching for the man who'd gone out of his way to make Tuesday evening so special for her and Kayla.

"Then how—" She swallowed and tried again. "Then how did you know I was with Tate?"

Mr. Borden cocked an eyebrow.

"Mrs. Applewhite told you?"

He nodded.

"What did she say?"

"That you and Tate had a picnic in the green space on Tuesday night."

A chill coursed through her veins. "Is that why she's been standoffish with me the past few days?"

"I'm afraid so. She thinks you're cavorting with the enemy."

Phoebe snorted. "You can't be serious."

He cocked an eyebrow once again.

"Oh." She leaned against the table and quietly surveyed the aftermath of their tag sale. Unwanted items, empty tables and colorful signs were strewn along the sidewalk as far as the eye could see. Remnants of their desperate race to save an age-old neighborhood treasure. Yet the same people who were hanging on to the good old days had turned their backs on one of their own.

A gentle finger under her chin forced her focus back to her elderly neighbor. "So why are you quiet? Is it Tate?"

"No. It's me." She sighed. "Or, rather, the me I'm not."

"I don't follow." Mr. Borden looked genuinely confused. "What could possibly be wrong with you?"

Phoebe crossed her arms and squinted at the afternoon sun. "I'm different than he is."

"Different?"

"In the same way I was different from Kayla's father." She grasped her grandmother's locket between her thumb and index finger and slid it back and forth on its delicate gold chain. "I wasn't raised around money, I didn't go to charm school, and to me, throwing a classy party means homemade cakes and apple pie, not French pastries and chocolate fountains."

"I'd take your cakes and pie over that fancy stuff any day of the week."

Tilting her head, she mustered a smile for her friend. "Of course you'd say that. You're kind and sweet and—"

"And I've been around the block a few times in my life, young lady." Mr. Borden dropped his forearms to the table. "The reason I'd take your kind of party over that highfalutin stuff is because nothing beats warmth and sincerity in my book. Nothing."

Phoebe glanced at Kayla, her voice beginning to tremble. "Not everyone has the same book, though."

Mr. Borden reached out, grasping her hand in his. "Then those are the books you leave on the shelf, Phoebe."

"But I know I could have—" she faltered momentarily before carrying on in a rush "—could have fit into Doug's world. I can do anything I put my mind to. Problem was, he didn't believe in me enough."

"His loss." The elderly man squeezed her hand until she met his eyes. "He gave up the best part of life when he turned his back on you and that little angel over there. And there is no doubt in my mind he will regret it one day."

"But Kayla lost, too."

"I don't agree." Mr. Borden waved in the baby's direction. "That is one happy and loved child. She's confident in her place in your life. If that man couldn't see past his prestige and fancy lifestyle to consider his own offspring, then she's better off without him."

"He offered to support us for life."

"Support and love are two different things. I admire you for turning him down. You and your daughter will be better off because of it." Mr. Borden pulled himself to his feet and grabbed his walker. "Will times be rough as a working mom? Sure. But you know we love you, and we'll all do what we can to help."

She could feel her eyes starting to tear up and she swallowed quickly. "I know. I couldn't have made it the past six months without all of you."

"Sure you could have. *We* couldn't have made it without the two of *you*." Mr. Borden started toward Kayla, then stopped. "But what does this all have to do with Tate?"

"I don't know. I guess it's this party he's taking me to tonight. It's at some fancy restaurant in West Cedarville and I'm afraid he'll think I don't fit in, either." Phoebe walked beside her neighbor to Kayla's play area.

"Let me tell you a few things, Phoebe." Mr. Borden stopped, gripping the bars of his walker tightly. "First of all, you carry yourself with grace. Have since the day I met you. You have a warmth inside you that radiates outward, drawing people to you whether you realize it or not. And last but not least, Tate Williams grew up right here on Quinton Lane. People don't forget their roots. He's going to see you for exactly who you are—a beautiful, sensitive, talented, warm and loving woman."

She tried to respond, to say something even semi-intelligent, but she was too stunned to do so. "I—I don't know what to say."

Mr. Borden leaned over his walker and kissed her temple. "Just say you'll be yourself. It's all you *can* be. And believe me, it's more than enough."

PHOEBE ADJUSTED the straps of her emerald-green silk camisole and twirled in front of the mirror, the knee-length black skirt swirling around her legs in a way that was sweet and sexy at the same time. Her hair had cooperated, tendrils escaping the French twist in just the right way to emphasize her high cheekbones. If she didn't know any better she'd think she dressed like this all the time.

But she *did* know better. Her daily attire consisted of jeans and paint smocks. Not silk tops and three-inch heels. And her normal dining consisted of macaroni and cheese and pizza, not lobster tails and filet mignon.

"Awww, Boots, what am I doing? I've been down this road once before. It didn't work then. Why should I think it could this time?" Phoebe sank onto the white, cushioned vanity bench across from her bed and sighed.

The cat, who'd been eyeing her lazily from on top of the bedspread throughout the impromptu fashion show, suddenly stood and walked over to the edge of the mattress, her big yellow eyes reflecting the light from the floor lamp.

"Yes?" Phoebe asked with as much playfulness as she could muster.

Boots simply looked at her then jumped onto the vanity, her tail weaving in front of a silver-framed photo Phoebe kept dead center.

Gram.

Phoebe inhaled quickly as her gaze fell on the woman who'd taught her everything she knew. About life. About love. About dreams. And about believing in herself—always. A five-star restaurant didn't change the fact that she was still Phoebe Jennings.

"Thanks, Boots," she whispered as she squared her shoulders and headed for the stairs.

Chapter Eleven

Tate knew Phoebe Jennings was a beautiful woman; he'd have to be blind not to see that. But still, he was unprepared for just how breathtaking she truly was when she greeted him that evening. The long legs that had tantalized him in shorts earlier in the week were downright dangerous emerging from underneath her black, slitted skirt and running all the way down to her black, strappy heels. Her virtually bare shoulders show-cased soft, lightly tanned skin his fingers begged to caress. But it was her khaki eyes, sparkling with antici-pation as she smiled, that made him moan inwardly with desire.

"You look incredible, Phoebe." He tried to keep his voice light and casual, but it was difficult. All day he'd been aware of the fact they'd be on their own that night for the first time, and his mind had run amok with images, with possibilities, unlikely as they were. Seeing her now, so vibrant and alive, only fanned the fire.

"Thanks, Tate. So do you."

He couldn't help but notice the way her eyes flick-ered across his face before traveling down his body, her cheeks taking on a pinkish hue as she caught him watching her.

"Would—would you like to come in for a moment?" she stammered. Her voice was quiet, almost shy, and it endeared her to him all the more.

Tate glanced down at his watch and swore silently to himself. As much as he'd love to take advantage of every moment possible, the reception was due to start in thirty minutes. And considering he was the guest of honor, it was probably best to hit the road. "I'd love to, but we'd better get going."

"Of course." Phoebe spun gracefully on her heels, grabbing a small black clutch from the antique table beside the door before joining him on the porch. As she turned the key in the lock and dropped it into her bag, she smiled up at him, wisps of hair curling delicately around her cheekbones. "It feels weird to be going somewhere without a diaper bag in tow. I guess it's been longer than I realized since I've had a grown-up night."

Her wistful look pulled at his heartstrings, and he ached to draw her into his arms and taste her lips. But he resisted. If all went well, there'd be time for that later.

Placing his hand against the small of her back, he guided her down the porch steps and along the sidewalk, his senses keenly aware of all things Phoebe Jennings. The feel of her silk top beneath his fingers. The scent of lilacs and summertime that seemed to float in the air around her...

And then there was the little matter of how his body was reacting to those subtleties.

"So where *is* your little angel this evening?" he asked as much out of curiosity as distraction.

"She's eating dinner at the Haskells'. When it's bedtime they'll bring her over here so she can sleep in her own crib." Phoebe gently touched his forearm as she stopped on the sidewalk to look at him. "They said we could stay out as long as we wanted, but I'd rather not take advantage, if that's okay."

"I understand. As long as we put in an appearance, enjoy our dinner and maybe take a spin or two around the dance floor, we can wrap it up whenever you want." He pulled the passenger door of his BMW open and admired her slender body as she lowered herself into the sports car. "Does Kayla do well with them?"

"The Haskells? Oh, yes. She adores them." Phoebe paused as he walked around the front of the car and slid into his spot behind the steering wheel. "Kayla is an easy baby. Very happy and cheerful. I have no problem painting when she's around. But I couldn't have worked all those parties in the evenings if it hadn't been for the Haskells' ongoing offer to watch her whenever I needed."

He turned the key in the ignition and shifted the car into gear, slowly pulling away from the curb. "How often do you work those parties?"

"I don't anymore. The Dolangers' event was my last. Thanks solely to the painting I did—ironically, for *them*. And if all goes well, I can make it from here on out just from my art. But it will be tight."

"You should open up a gallery in West Cedarville. You'd make a killing."

Her sweet laughter filled the car and he smiled instantly. "What's so funny?"

She raised an eyebrow. "A gallery in West Cedarville? I don't think so. Not unless Kayla and I were to live on the streets. And even then it wouldn't work."

"What do you mean?" He turned onto Route 52 and headed toward the western edge of town.

"Making rent for my house isn't always easy. Leasing a building in downtown West Cedarville could never happen."

"Do you know how many people on that side of town will be tripping over themselves to commission you to paint portraits of *their* family now? You could rent five buildings."

He glanced across the seat, his smile disappearing as he realized she was looking down at her hands. "Phoebe? You okay?"

"I'm fine." She pulled her focus from her lap and fixed it instead on the passing scenery. "So, this dinner has something to do with your work?"

Unsure of what to make of the sudden and seemingly deliberate shift in conversation, he simply nodded and pointed out the window. "Do you see that place? The one up there on the bluff? A colleague at another firm designed it, and it's supposed to be incredible. Eight bedrooms, six bathrooms, a rec room that would make any guy salivate, a media room, an indoor swimming pool, separate guest quarters—you get the idea. Should be close to three million by the time all is said and done."

"That's a lot of house for one family."

"Even more for just one guy." Tate swung his attention back to the road in time to see the sign for their exit.

"You can't be serious?"

"Trust me, I am. He's West Cedarville's newest and most eligible bachelor and likes to entertain the ladies in style, from what I hear. I met him a few months ago at some party." Tate pulled onto the ramp, slowing his speed to accommodate the upcoming traffic signal. "Unfortunately, it was more or less a quick hi, hello kind of thing. Which means the chance of scoring a behind-the-scenes tour of his new digs is slim to none."

"Do you like homes like that?" she asked.

"Sure. Doesn't everyone?" He made a quick left on Tower Grove Avenue, then an immediate right onto Linley Street. Pedestrians were out in full force, enjoying the warm evening, peeking in shop windows and dining in outdoor cafés.

As the Autumn Room, with its slender white columns and lighted trees, came into view, he looked at his date once again. The genuine happiness he'd seen on Phoebe's face when he'd arrived at her door had dissipated somewhat, replaced by an aura of uncertainty, maybe even sadness. His stomach turned.

"Everything okay?" He stopped the car at the curb and waved to the impeccably dressed attendant at the valet stand. As the man hurried in their direction, Tate took a moment to reach across the center console and gently guide her chin until their eyes met. "You seem...I don't know...*sad,* maybe?"

"Just a little tired, I guess. Tag sales are quite a lot of excitement, you know?" She flashed a reassuring smile in his direction before grabbing her clutch purse and exiting the car as the valet opened her door.

"Did it go well?" Tate asked as he, too, got out of the car, then hurried around to her side.

"Very well. We raised close to a thousand dollars, if you can believe it. Though that won't buy us more than a few young trees, I'm afraid."

Tucking her hand in his arm, he walked with her toward the glass door trimmed in miniature white lights. "A few new trees would be a really nice addition, as long as they don't interfere with a potential Whiffle ball game or impromptu round of hide-and-seek."

Her laugh echoed through the vestibule, warming his heart. "I'm not sure there's anyone left who has the energy for such play. Though I'm sure Kayla will be revved and ready to go in a few short years."

"Well, see, there you go. Trees are good, just be careful where you put them."

"Unfortunately, I'm not terribly confident a few trees will be enough to satisfy the city, and the Quinton Lane crowd doesn't have a lot of money to invest in something bigger."

He glanced down at her, his breath nearly catching at the way she looked up at him with a mixture of concern for her friends and anticipation of…*their evening together?* He wasn't sure, but he was hopeful. "I think we'll make them happy."

"I don't follow," she said, her voice becoming harder to hear as they walked toward the second set of doors and the band playing inside.

"I think we'll find a way to please the city and get them to go sniffing around some other part of town."

"We?"

Raising a finger to the tip of her nose, he gave her a mischievous smile. "Come on, there's someone I want you to meet."

He laughed as she protested, "Uh-uh! You can't leave me hanging like that…"

"I can. And I just did." Gently, he untucked her hand from his arm and grasped it with his own, pulling her toward the private room his firm had reserved for the night. He was proud to have Phoebe Jennings on his arm, excited to show her off to his partners, eager to introduce her to Regina in a more relaxed atmosphere than a brief exchange outside his office had afforded.

Band music wafted from the end of the hall, beckoning them inside. A man dressed impeccably in a crisp white shirt and black suit greeted them. "Your name, sir?"

"Tate Williams."

The man's face lit up. "Mr. Williams, we're so glad you've arrived. And we're honored that you would celebrate such a special occasion with us here at the Autumn Room." He motioned them through, alerting a server on the other side to their arrival. "Serina will be available to take care of anything you or your guest may need this evening. Congratulations on your accomplishment, Mr. Williams."

"Thank you." Tate released Phoebe's hand, placing his own at the small of her back as he guided her through the crowd of people who, one by one, noticed their arrival and turned to clap.

"What's going on?" she whispered. "You didn't tell me this was for *you*."

"I guess that's not the part I was focused on when I asked you to come with me."

"So what did you do?"

"I've been named partner at my firm. McDonald and

Murphy will, from here on out, be known as McDonald, Murphy and Williams Architectural Firm."

"Are you serious?"

He grinned. "Yup."

"I think that was an important piece of information, don't you?"

"Nah. The important part was your saying yes to my invitation. The rest was easy."

The way she shook her head in mock disgust made him laugh out loud and he pulled her closer as they threaded their way through the maze of guests, stopping from time to time to shake a hand and offer introductions. Each and every time, Phoebe's face brightened with a genuine smile, her warmth putting everyone at ease.

Finally they reached the other side of the room where Regina was waiting, her arms outstretched for a hug. Tate removed his hand from Phoebe's back long enough to embrace his secretary.

"Regina, you remember Phoebe Jennings, don't you? And Phoebe, my secretary extraordinaire and even better friend, Regina Melvey?"

The women gravitated toward each other immediately, as if their brief encounter at his office had lasted years rather than moments. It didn't surprise him, since they were alike in many ways—hardworking, genuine, caring, funny…

"I understand you're an artist, Phoebe?" Regina motioned to a few empty chairs positioned around a table in a quiet corner of the bustling room. "I've always admired creative people. Writers. Actors. Architects. Painters. It's such a gift."

Tate leaned back in his chair and simply watched and listened as the two women shared a little about themselves. There were so many things he'd noticed about Phoebe over the past two weeks that had embedded themselves in his thoughts. The way her smile spread across her face, enhanced by the sparkle in her eyes. The way she cocked her head a hairbreadth to the left as she listened… The way she downplayed her talent…

"My dream has always been to open a studio," she was saying. "For portraits mainly, but certainly not exclusively. It's just that capturing a person or family at a distinct moment in time has always interested me."

A waiter appeared behind them, a large tray of caviar hors d'oeuvres in his hand. He held it toward Tate.

"Phoebe? Regina?"

The women shook their heads in unison, then laughed.

"Not your thing, either?" Regina asked with amusement.

"No." Phoebe leaned back in her seat and tickled Tate's arm, his skin tingling at her touch. "I'm more of a mini hot dog and cheese cube kind of girl."

"Me, too," he said.

"Really?" She glanced in his direction, then playfully rolled her eyes at Regina.

"What?" He started to cross his arms, then realized what he'd said. "Wait. Me, too. On all but the girl part, anyway."

"That's a relief." Regina turned toward a female server, who appeared with a tray of wine goblets. "What kind is that, dear?"

As the two discussed the various selections of wine, Tate rubbed his hand slowly across Phoebe's bare arm, acutely aware of how she blushed in response. "Having fun?"

"Yes. Regina is wonderful." She looked at his secretary quickly, then leaned close to his ear. "She's someone I could talk to for hours."

"I know. Trust me. I've lost many valuable hours of work time doing just that. But I'm going to pry you two apart soon so I can dance with you." He gave her arm a gentle squeeze. "You look beautiful tonight and I don't want to share you the whole time."

Regina took a sip of her chosen wine, then took charge of the conversation once again. "You have a daughter, Phoebe?"

She nodded and smiled. "Kayla. She's eleven months old."

"It must be hard being on your own with someone so small."

Surprised by Regina's directness, Tate sat up in his chair, ready to change the subject at a moment's notice. But if Phoebe was bothered by the question, she didn't let it show.

"It is at times. Like when Kayla is sick and I have to work. Or when she wants cuddle time and I'm facing a deadline. But somehow it always works out. Some of that, I think, is the angel we have looking over us."

"Angel?"

"My grandmother. She died two years ago. She was my grandmother, grandfather, mother, father and best friend all rolled into one. And she always believed in me, no matter what."

Tate glanced over at Regina. "Sounds like someone in *my* life." Then he turned toward Phoebe and placed his hand atop hers. "And I can't imagine anyone *not* believing in you."

The sparkle in her eyes disappeared almost immediately, replaced by a flash of pain. "Kayla's father didn't." The words were no sooner out of her mouth than her cheeks reddened. "I'm sorry. I shouldn't have said that. It's not the time or the place for such things."

Regina shook her head. "In what way did he not believe in you?"

Once again, his secretary's straightforwardness took Tate by surprise though it shouldn't have. It was one of the things he admired most about her. She cut to the chase. Always.

"Kayla's father was from a very wealthy family. The multigenerational kind of wealth. My grandmother did everything she could to keep a roof over my head—babysitting, making quilts, tutoring, you name it. Doug and I were as opposite as two people could be in terms of upbringing. Monetary upbringing, anyway."

"So how did you end up together?"

"I think the fact that I was different from anything he'd ever known is why he gravitated toward me. I was an unknown, I guess. We dated through the latter part of college and after graduation. Eventually I got pregnant with Kayla, and that's when things changed. When the differences between us became an issue."

"You mean the fact he had money?" Tate asked.

She nodded. "No longer would he be able to just take me to movies or out to eat. If we got married and had a child, I'd have to be a part of his real world. A world with important people and fancy parties. A world where women stayed home and spent their days checking in on the nanny and chairing various charity events. A world he didn't think I could fit into."

"So he left you and your child?" The disbelief in Regina's voice mirrored the sentiment in Tate's heart.

Again, Phoebe nodded. "He wanted to pretend we didn't exist. So it would be less messy. He offered to support us for life. He just didn't want us to be a part of his, or to have any part of ours."

"Wait. I knew it didn't work out…but this guy tried to buy you off?" Tate heard the incredulousness in his voice, saw a few nearby heads turn in their direction.

Phoebe shifted uncomfortably, her own voice dropping to a near whisper. "Sadly, yes."

"But you've been working two jobs, worrying about rent." He felt his face growing warm with anger.

"That's because I told him no. If he didn't want to be a part of our lives, didn't believe I could fit into his, I wanted no part of his offer."

"Good for you," Regina said, folding her arms across her chest in solidarity.

"But he *owed* you that much," Tate insisted.

"Maybe. But I want Kayla to believe she's worth more in life. And the only way to show her that is to demonstrate it." Phoebe looked down at the table. "It's not easy. But it's right."

"Does he see her at all?" Tate was having difficulty wrapping his mind around Phoebe's story.

"No. He wanted a clean split. Felt it was better for everyone that way." When she glanced up again, a sober look replaced the happiness of earlier. "I feel bad for Kayla sometimes. But she deserves better. I know that."

"You're damn right she does," he declared angrily,

then felt Regina's hand on his shoulder. "I'm sorry, it's just—"

"It's okay," Phoebe interrupted, a slow smile appearing across her face. "Life goes on. For me and for Kayla. We don't need Doug Rider in our lives."

Regina's gasp was all the confirmation Tate needed that he had, indeed, heard the correct name. "Did you say *Doug Rider?*"

Phoebe nodded. "Why? Do you know him?"

Tate set his elbow on the table in front of them and ran a hand through his hair. "Yeah. I met him at a few parties over the past few months. He's the guy building that house I showed you."

"The three-million-dollar one?" she asked with a frown, as if grappling to make the connection. But if she was angry or hurt, it didn't show.

"Yeah."

For several long minutes they sat in silence, the party continuing around them. Couples danced, business associates conversed, the waitstaff hustled to and fro, filling drinks and offering appetizers from over-flowing trays.

It was incomprehensible to Tate how someone could walk away from his own child and show no desire to meet her or be part of her life. He wanted to say something, anything, to make it right, but there was nothing he could say. No way to explain the unexplainable.

The lull was soon broken by Phoebe's sweet voice, happy and sure. "That's okay. He can have his mansion. I'll take Quinton Lane any day of the week. We're loved there. Truly loved. And that's worth more than any fancy rec room or indoor pool."

"But you have to work so hard," he interjected, the frustration he felt evident in each word.

"You're right, I do. But it's par for the course when you're reaching for a dream. If dreams came easily they wouldn't be so special."

Regina reached across the table and patted Phoebe's hand. "Your world sounds a whole lot better to me."

"Thank you." She flashed a smile at his secretary, then slowly scanned the crowd of partygoers before finally turning her khaki-green eyes to meet his. "It's the *only* world where I truly fit."

Chapter Twelve

Phoebe leaned her head against the seat back and closed her eyes, the corners of her mouth tilting upward at the memory of dancing in Tate's arms, his body pressed against hers. The yearning in his eyes had mirrored her own, she knew. It had been a long time since she'd felt even a *hint* of interest for a man, let alone the all-out desire she felt for Tate Williams.

And it scared her.

Sure, there were as many differences between Tate and Doug as there were similarities. But the biggest commonality the two men shared was also the very thing that had made Kayla's dad run for the hills.

Lifestyle. Or, more aptly stated, money.

"I loved having you there tonight. It made the promotion a million times more special."

She opened her eyes at the feel of Tate's finger on her jaw and turned to look at him as they sped along Route 52 on the way back to Quinton Lane. "You really mean that, don't you?"

"I wouldn't say it if I didn't." He grasped her hand in his, their forearms resting side by side on the center console. "I wasn't wild about the idea of a party when Regina gave me the heads-up, but then I figured it might be a chance to spend some time with you."

Phoebe looked down at his fingers entwined with hers, and felt her body begin to hum. The tenderness he conveyed in a simple touch of her face was something she wanted to experience elsewhere—along other parts of her body.

"Why wouldn't you want to celebrate?" she asked, desperate to steer her thoughts from the path they were hurtling down.

"I'm not a party sort of guy. Not that stuffy kind, anyway."

She snapped her head up. *"Stuffy?"*

"Yeah." He glanced quickly to his left and switched lanes. "You know what I mean. The caviar, the wine… the pastries that are more about looks than taste."

"But you said at your office the other day that you attend these kinds of parties often."

"I do. Because of my job. But that doesn't mean I like them."

What he'd said matched her own feelings.

"My mom, on the other hand, could throw one heck of a party. Homemade lasagna, cold cuts, chicken wings, brownies and beer. God, I miss those. Miss the atmosphere. Miss the genuine conversations and multifaceted people." His voice trailed off and his mouth set in an unreadable expression.

The sentiment didn't come as a surprise when Phoebe thought back over the evening. While polite and friendly with everyone at the party, Tate seemed to return again and again to Regina, a move Phoebe now realized was as much about his comfort zone as it was anything else.

"Once a Quinton Laner, always a Quinton Laner...."

Mr. Borden's words paraded through her thoughts, reminding her that, unlike Doug, Tate hadn't grown up around money. A fact that might serve to balance the difference between his current lifestyle and hers.

"Pizza and brownies?" she asked playfully. "You just described a Quinton Lane party to a T. All except the beer part, anyway—now it's energy drinks and V8."

"I wouldn't know." He turned off the highway and headed toward the older section of Cedarville, the stars in the black sky twinkling overhead. "The day my mom died is the day I fell off that invite list once and for all. But in all fairness, I probably wasn't on it for a number of years before that, either.... She just foisted me on them. Tried to, anyway. I always found an excuse not to attend, and I suspect they were thrilled I did."

Her heart ached for the pain and betrayal he still felt from a misunderstanding that had happened years earlier. "I suspect most of them realize they were in the wrong." She peered at him as he pulled to a stop outside her home, noted the way his jaw tightened as he turned off the engine.

"Let's let sleeping dogs lie. Besides, tonight has been too magical to end on such a sour note." She saw him swallow, heard the pleading in his voice, felt the desire in his touch as he leaned across the console and kissed her ever so gently. "Any chance I could take you up on that offer you made earlier? The one about coming in for a little while?"

Reaching up, she skimmed the back of her hand

across his cheek, wanting desperately to taste his lips again. "I'd like that."

The air around them was heavy with desire as they walked up the steps to her front door. She wanted him, plain and simple. But she was also smart enough to know that was her body talking.

Tate Williams was handsome, intelligent, sweet, kind and incredibly sexy. He could make her knees grow weak with a single look, her body tingle with an innocent touch. But the world he inhabited made her hesitate, caused her internal radar to flash.

Her hand was trembling as she pulled her house key from her purse and inserted it into the lock. If he noticed, he didn't comment, and she was grateful. The last thing she wanted to do was try and sort through her jumbled feelings right then and there.

Pushing the door open, she stepped into the foyer and motioned for Tate to follow. The downward cast of his eyes caught her by surprise. Had she misread his request to come inside?

"Hello, dear. Did you have fun?"

Phoebe smiled at her neighbor. "Oh, I did. It was wonderful. Thank you so much for watching Kayla so I could go." She glanced again at Tate, noted the slight rigidity in his posture—and suddenly understood the reason. "Mrs. Haskell, you remember Tate Williams, don't you?"

He looked up, a curious mixture of apprehension and hope on his face as he waited for the woman's reply.

"Of course I do. Tate and John were good friends for a very long time. How are you, dear?"

A slow smile appeared across his face as he accepted

the woman's gentle hug. "I'm doing well, thank you. I appreciate you watching Phoebe's little princess so she could come with me tonight."

Mrs. Haskell reached around the corner and retrieved her book from an end table. "My pleasure. Kayla is an absolute joy." The woman grasped Phoebe's hand in hers and lowered her voice a notch. "She seemed to be having a little trouble with her gums as the evening wore on, and I gave her a little Tylenol before bed. I haven't heard a peep from her since."

"Thank you." Phoebe walked her neighbor to the door and watched until she was safely down the road before turning off the porch light. Slowly, she turned around, her heart thumping at the realization that she and Tate were virtually alone. It had been ages since she'd been with a man in any way.

"Come with me," he said, his voice husky. Turning on his heel, he led her into the family room and over to the couch.

"Would you like something to drink? I actually bought a bottle of wine at the store last night." She knew she sounded nervous, yet couldn't seem to calm herself enough to act naturally.

He shook his head as he sat, then pulled her down beside him. "I just want to spend a little quiet time with you."

The thumping of her heart increased as the sides of their bodies brushed together, first unintentionally, then quite deliberately. The heat emanating from his skin was unmistakable, and it made her want him even more.

Leaning forward just enough to make eye contact, he cupped her face in his hands. "This is all I've wanted since you showed up at my door two weeks ago, ready to play post master."

She searched his golden-brown eyes for something that would warn her off—a hint of evil, a snatch of arrogance, anything. But if it was there, she wasn't seeing it. She was simply *feeling*—the warmth of his skin, the firmness of his touch, the intense longing as his lips closed on hers, the eager probing of his tongue....

Suddenly she wasn't Phoebe Jennings, rejected lover, any longer. She was simply a woman with an intense need to know Tate Williams in a way she hadn't known another man in a very long time. And as their kiss intensified, she slid her arms around his back, reveling in the feel of his muscles beneath her fingers and the sensation of his hands in her hair, pulling her head back so he could kiss her chin, her neck, the base of her throat.

When his mouth reached the strap of her silk camisole, he stopped to look at her as if seeking permission to continue. She said nothing, choosing instead to let her eyes tell him everything he needed to know.

With a gentle, yet deliberate finger, Tate slid one strap, then the other, from her shoulders, his gaze lingering on her chest as the camisole slipped to her waist, revealing the skimpy, black lace bra underneath. He moaned, then bowed his head to continue exploring her skin with his lips, while his hands found her breasts.

"Oh, Tate," she whispered as he unfastened the clasp of her bra and pushed the fabric from her breasts. In an instant his mouth was on one, and then the other, his tongue teasing her nipples as they hardened with desire.

Reluctantly, he released her breast and looked up at

her as she nudged the bottom of his chin. "Let's go upstairs," she whispered.

As she stood, he took hold of her camisole and slid it up and off her body, her bra falling to the floor. Clad only in her black skirt and heels, she led him toward the stairs.

"God, you are beautiful, Phoebe Jennings," he murmured against her ear as he pulled her to him at the foot of the steps.

Her fingers found the buttons of his shirt and slowly undid each one, giving her hands free rein of his muscular chest. She looked up at him, felt an electric charge run through her body at the naked longing in his eyes.

For her.

Somehow they found their way up the stairs and past Kayla's closed door. Found their way into Phoebe's room and over to the bed. Silently, Tate sat on the edge of the mattress and pulled her toward him. Slowly, methodically, he unfastened her skirt and watched it fall to the floor, a look of sheer admiration on his face as he eyed her bare legs and black lace panties.

She wanted nothing more than to know this man completely. To give herself to him in every sense of the word. Boldly, she reached over and undid his pants, felt the most intimate parts of herself growing wet with desire at the sight of his body craning toward hers.

He pulled her to him, their heat mingling as he laid her down and lowered himself to her, their bodies joining effortlessly. She felt his length inside her, straining against her, and her head began to spin as their breathing slowly synchronized. Again and again they moved in rhythm, the heady sensations intensifying until they couldn't resist any longer, and gave in together.

HE WOKE TO THE SOUND of happy chatter and the smell of bacon frying. Slowly, Tate turned his head and looked at the indent in the pillow beside his own, recalling the way they'd made love again and again throughout the night, their bodies craving one another with an undeniable force.

Phoebe Jennings was an amazing lover. She was sweet and warm, adventurous yet shy, tender and giving. But it was the way she looked at him as he thrust into her that solidified what he'd been feeling with growing intensity all week.

He'd fallen in love with a woman who'd shown up at his door simply to deliver a letter. A woman who took time from her busy schedule to right someone else's wrong. Who saw a task through to completion. Who cared about the people in her world and brightened a room simply by cntcring it. A woman who walked away from the easy life in favor of teaching her daughter a lesson about dreams and pride.

A woman he couldn't wait to see.

Swinging his feet to the floor, Tate pushed himself off the bed and grabbed for the suit pants peeking out from the pile of Phoebe's clothing. He looked around for his shirt, grinning as he recalled the moment she'd peeled it from his chest.

The babble from downstairs grew louder as he took the steps two at a time, snatching his shirt from the hall table and shrugging into it as he headed toward the kitchen. He rounded the corner and stopped, a sense of comfort resonating through him at the sight of Phoebe and Kayla chatting at the table.

Suddenly he knew, without a doubt, what had been missing from his life for so long. It wasn't the next architectural success. It wasn't the understanding of his old neighbors. It wasn't a group he could be comfortable hanging out with.

It was *this*.

A family.

"I—I—I." Kayla's tiny hand shot into the air as she spotted him watching them from the doorway.

"Hi yourself, sweetie." He puffed out his chest in mock pride as Phoebe looked over her shoulder, her smile so beautiful it nearly took his breath away. "See? I'm a quick learner."

She lowered her eyebrows in confusion.

"Baby talk. She just said hi."

"Uh, no. That meant she needs a diaper change." Phoebe stood up and crossed the distance between them in a few short steps.

He felt deflated. "Really?"

"No." Phoebe wrapped her arms around his neck and cuddled against him, her lips warm against his ear as she whispered a naughty greeting not suitable for all ages.

Growling quietly, he kissed her temple. "Mmm. Okay, *that* greeting more than makes up for your teasing just now."

"Good." She stepped backward and motioned to the empty chair. "I just finished making some pancakes and bacon. I figured you might be a bit famished this morning."

"Dancing always does that," he quipped, tapping the tip of her nose with his index finger as her mouth opened in protest.

"Dancing, huh?"

"Among other things." Tate sat down and slowly walked his fingers across the table and onto Kayla's high chair tray. As they found a Cheerio, he popped it in his mouth, gobbling it as loudly as possible to the delight of the little girl. "Yum, yum, I'm *hungry* this morning."

Eventually the requests for an encore died out and he dived into his own breakfast, alternating bites with conversation that ran the gamut from Phoebe's next art project to his dreams for his career. He talked about his mother's belief in his abilities, and Phoebe did the same about her grandmother. And in the end, when the last pancake was gone, he couldn't help but feel even closer to this woman than he already did.

"Let's do something special today. Just the three of us." He grabbed both plates and put them in the sink despite her protests. "You made the meal. I will wash the dishes. It's only fair. You do far too much on your own as it is."

"Thank you."

"So? What shall it be? The zoo? Another picnic? A bike ride on the trail? You do have a baby seat for the back of your bike, right?" He squirted some dish soap on the plates.

"No, I don't. I've always wanted one, but it wasn't a priority." Phoebe ran a wet paper towel across Kayla's sticky mouth and hands, then lifted her from the chair for a quick cuddle and kiss before releasing her. "But even if I did, we—"

"We can just swing by one of the bike shops down by the trail and pick one up for her. It's good exercise and I'm betting she'd love it." He dried the plates carefully, then stacked them on the counter. "I could swing home real quick, grab some shorts and a T-shirt."

As Kayla squealed and crawled off in the direction of the family room, Phoebe wiped off the high chair cushion and tray and pushed in their chairs. "You're right, she'd love a bike ride, and your offer to get a baby seat is very generous. It's just we have plans for the afternoon, and I wouldn't feel right breaking them at this late notice."

"Oh." Tate folded the dish towel and secured it around the handle of the oven before turning to face her, hoping the delay would give him a moment to mask his disappointment. "I shouldn't have been so presumptuous. I'm sorry."

He felt her fingers on his face, then her lips on his, and the sudden tension disappeared as quickly as it had come. "It's not presumptuous. It's sweet. And if I hadn't made this commitment, we'd have loved spending the whole day with you." She stepped back and glanced down at her hands, her lips quivering slightly. "Breakfast just now was—" she swallowed and looked back at him, a hint of moisture in her eyes "—special. Kayla and I always have fun together, but this was different."

Gathering Phoebe into his arms, Tate held her close, reveling in the feel of her breath against the base of his throat as he kissed her hair. "I know what you mean. Since my mom died I've had no one. The women I've dated have left me cold, which is why I rarely had second dates with any of them. Regina is great and we spend a lot of time talking, but she's a friend. I miss that family feeling."

"You don't have to, you know. There's someone who

misses you very much and wants to be part of your life." Her words were barely discernable as her lips moved against his skin.

He gripped her shoulders gently and held her back just enough to see her face. "I missed that. What did you say?"

A hint of red appeared in her cheeks as she stammered, "You—you still have your dad, Tate. And he loves you."

He stared at her, shaking his head doggedly, saying words he didn't want to hear.

"When I delivered his letter, we talked. For a long time. He's a wonderful man, Tate. He loves you and misses you, and is living with more regret than anyone should have to. I just know you two can fix whatever went wrong if you simply take the time to talk…and then move forward. Gram used to say life is too short to live in the past—that's there for the memories. Life is about *living*. It's about today and tomorrow."

Dropping his hands, he strode toward the hallway and back, his shoulders rigid, his facial muscles tense.

She carried on, her voice taking on an almost pleading tone. "Last night, when I told you I suspected most of my neighbors know they were wrong in accusing you of selling the neighborhood out, I said that for good reason. Do you know that your father went to bat for you after your mom died? Told them they'd been wrong?"

"Did *he* tell you that?" Tate barked.

"No. Mr. Borden did."

Tate stopped in his tracks, ran his hands through his hair and then rubbed his face furiously.

"Your dad has been very lonely. He seems hell-bent

on punishing himself for everything. You could just feel the hurt and the sadness seeping from his soul despite the smile he was determined to wear." She pried Tate's hands from his face and held them gently. "At first I felt awful for giving him that letter—it stirred up so much pain and regret. But then, when I found her and put them in touch, it seemed to make such a difference. His voice this week on the phone was so hopeful."

"Found *her?* What are you talking about, Phoebe?"

"Lorraine. The woman who wrote him that letter nearly forty years ago. Before either you or I were born."

"Lorraine?" He knew his tone was stiff, biting even, but it was all he could do not to yell at the top of his lungs.

Phoebe nodded, her eyes wide with excitement. "Yes. Lorraine Walters. The woman he'd proposed to while overseas. Her letter got lost and he assumed her answer was a no and—"

"He proposed to someone before my mother?" Tate pulled his hands from hers, his feet moving backward, his mind reeling from the implications of what he was hearing.

"Yes, but—"

"And you put them in contact? Again?"

The excitement in her eyes disappeared and fear took its place. "Yes, but don't you see, it's—"

"I see nothing except a woman who stuck her nose where it didn't belong, all so she could have her perfect storybook ending…no matter what the cost to those around her." He turned on his heel and stormed into the hallway, narrowly missing Kayla as she crawled in the direction of his raised voice and her mother's teary pleas.

"Tate! Wait. Please. Hear me out!" Phoebe called.

"There's so much you need to hear, so much more your father can explain."

He whirled around to face her, his lips pulled downward with rage. "*My* father?" He saw Kayla scoot backward, her face contort with fear, her eyes fill with tears, but he kept going, unable to stop the anger that was building inside him. "You mean the man who barely showed my mother an ounce of affection in nearly thirty years of marriage? The man who was more than content to watch my childhood from a recliner in the family room or from behind a newspaper on the front porch? *That's* the guy you mean, right? *My father?* The guy who stood by and watched an entire neighborhood all but tar and feather me for something I had no control over?"

Any glimmer of hope that he'd misread his father for all those years, any chance Regina was right when she encouraged him to give his dad another chance, had been wiped out the moment Lorraine Walters's name was mentioned.

His father *had* been disinterested in them all those years. And now Tate knew why.

He and his mom hadn't been Bart Williams's first choice for a family.

"Tate, it's not like that. Just hear me out. Please!"

He stood there in the hallway, his eyes moving from Kayla's terrified face to Phoebe's red and swollen eyes, the reality of his upbringing tearing away every ounce of progress he'd made in moving forward in his life.

And it was all because of some damn letter…

Shaking his head, he turned his back to them and headed for the door, slamming it behind him as he left 2565 Quinton Lane for the very last time.

Chapter Thirteen

Despite Phoebe's attempts to be happy and playful, it was obvious Kayla wasn't fooled. Phoebe was hurting, deeply, and there was no faking her way out of that—even with an eleven-month-old.

"Ma-maaa."

For the umpteenth time since Tate had stormed out of their home, Kayla reached her pudgy hands up to Phoebe's eyes, a worried expression on her little face.

"It's okay, sweetie. Mommy's just fine." But when Kayla popped her thumb into her mouth and leaned her head on Phoebe's shoulder, she knew her words were as hollow as they sounded.

Damn you, Tate Williams.

Never in her life had she met a man who was as pig-headed and shortsighted as Tate.

Or as tender and loving.

Swallowing over the ever-present lump in her throat, Phoebe hoisted Kayla higher on her hip and turned the last corner, then fixed her eyes on Bart's American flag. If there were any elderly women getting their hair done in the center's salon, she didn't notice.

Watching Tate walk out her door just hours after making love had been painful enough. Reminders of her grandmother, at a time Phoebe desperately needed her love and guidance, would be nothing short of crushing.

When they reached Bart's door, she stopped, looked down at Kayla and kissed her soft temple. "Let's have a nice visit, okay, baby girl?"

"A."

Out popped the thumb and up went the head as Kayla peered at the closed door in anticipation, squealing with genuine glee as Phoebe's knock was promptly answered.

"Would you look at who's here." Bart's low voice boomed into the hallway and a smile spread across his face as he reached out to tweak Kayla's nose. "I've been looking forward to your visit all day and now here you are."

The toddler clapped her hands together and kicked her feet against Phoebe's thighs.

"Whoa, little lady, be gentle with your mama." Bart stepped to the side and motioned them inside. "I picked up a box of blocks the other day at the store. Think she'll like those?"

Taking a breath, Phoebe answered with as much enthusiasm as she could muster. "She'll love them. Thank you." She'd almost made it—and *would* have if she hadn't added the last two words. Somehow, acknowledging Bart's thoughtfulness made her voice crack.

"You okay, Phoebe?" His hand, wrinkled and leathery, touched her forearm as he searched her face. "Your eyes look sad."

She nibbled her lower lip and shook her head, afraid to open her mouth for fear of letting her emotions rise to the surface. Bart didn't need to know just how much his son despised him. What good could come from that?

Aware of him watching her every move, she carried Kayla over to the blanket he'd laid out on the floor, the brand-new building blocks carefully placed in the center.

"Look, Kayla. Blocks!" She bent over and placed the baby on the blanket, taking a moment to stack three blocks before leaving her to explore on her own. "How kind of you to remember Kayla while you were at the store."

"I've thought of little else since your visit." Bart shuffled around the sofa and lowered himself slowly to the floor. "Meeting the two of you was a wonderful treat. Then, when I realized you were coming back, I started eyeing the calendar. That's what us old farts do, you know."

Phoebe laughed, a sound that echoed through the tiny room. Kayla looked up and smiled, a block in each hand.

"*There* it is," Bart said with pleasure.

"What?"

"Your smile. And apparently I wasn't the only one who noticed it was lacking its normal sparkle." He reached across the blanket and patted Kayla on the head. "This little girl may not have a terribly big vocabulary yet, but she understands more than you realize."

Phoebe let his words swirl around in her head as she perched on the edge of the sofa. "You seem to be very good with babies. Were you close to your son?"

She knew the question was unfair, especially when she knew more about his background than he realized, but she let it stand nonetheless. She'd been on the receiving end of some bitter statements on the matter and was more than curious as to their validity.

The ensuing silence, coupled with the downward

turn of Bart's mouth, said more than any reply ever could. It was clear that the relationship between the Williams men was a source of heartache for both.

Eventually, the elderly man spoke, putting words to the raw emotion evident in both his expression and his posture. "I loved my son in a way I've never loved anyone or anything. He was a joy from the moment he was born. Curious. Sensitive. Athletic. Intelligent. Driven. Loving. But I watched it from afar. All of it. Because of that damn hurt I carried."

"Over Lorraine?" Phoebe looked down at her lap and her fidgeting fingers.

"Yes. I was so haunted by the—the not knowing and the rejection that I...I held myself back from Tate's mother." He waved his hand in the air, then grabbed a pile of blocks. "I told you all this the other day and I don't want to bore you with my tale of woe. But I always felt undeserving of Mary and her love, a feeling I guess I put onto Tate, as well. I felt he deserved better in a father. That he deserved a man who would love his mother the way she deserved."

Phoebe considered her next question before expressing it aloud. "Do you have any regrets?"

"What *don't* I regret about that time?" Slowly, he placed one block atop the other, forcing a surprised expression when Kayla knocked them down. "I don't regret marrying Mary. I don't regret having Tate. But I regret everything else. They were gifts I should have treasured. And in many ways I think I did.... I just did so inside, out of some misplaced fear of rejection. I think I was afraid to ever give my heart as completely as I did with Lorraine, for fear it would be stolen and trampled again…the way I thought it had been already. But I'd give anything, *anything,* to do those years over with Mary, to make things right with Tate."

Phoebe felt excitement beginning to well up in her body, a plan starting to form. Tate might never speak to her again, but if she could find a way to get the two men together, at least something good would have come from their paths crossing.

"You still feel that way about Mary and Tate even knowing you could have been with Lorraine, after all?"

He nodded, a single tear glistening in the corner of each eye. "I've asked myself that same question over and over since you delivered that letter. And you know what? I don't believe the letter getting lost was a coincidence. I was *meant* to be with Mary at that time in my life. Lorraine was meant for *now.*"

Although her mind was already concocting a way to get the men together, Bart's words snapped her back to the here and now. "So you've talked?"

A flash of red appeared in his cheeks and he turned away long enough to clear his throat. "Several times a day, *every* day, since you gave her my number."

Phoebe was happy for the man who sat on the blanket with her daughter, a smile on his face now after a difficult trip down memory lane. Life was too short to spend it looking backward. It was meant to be lived. Cherished.

If she'd held on to Doug's betrayal, she never would have had her night with Tate. And although it ended the way it had, she wouldn't trade that experience for anything. The hours alone with him had been magical, making her feel alive for the first time in nearly two years.

Leaning down, she squeezed Bart's shoulder. "I'm so

happy for the two of you, I truly am. When do you think you'll actually meet?"

A mischievous twinkle appeared in his eye as he looked down at the floor and then back at her. "We already have. We had dinner together on Friday night, lunch together yesterday, and we have plans to go to the history museum tomorrow afternoon and to the unveiling of the Innovation House on Wednesday."

"Innovation House?"

"It's a home that's designed by a local architect, built by a local builder and decorated by a variety of different interior designers from the area. Once it's completed, you buy tickets to tour the inside. The money raised goes to a particular charity. Eventually the home is auctioned off to the highest bidder. Lorraine is on the committee for the Multiple Sclerosis Association—this year's chosen charity."

"I'm so very glad you and Lorraine found each other again. It gives me goose bumps just thinking about it." And it did. Never, in all her daydreaming about the origins of the letter, had she imagined it would reunite old lovers.

"I am, too. But none of it would have happened without you." He struggled to his feet, pulling her from her spot on the edge of the sofa. "*You* made it happen, Phoebe. And I am forever indebted to you for that."

She closed her eyes as he embraced her, the irony of his words touching off the heartbreak she'd managed to push aside long enough to enjoy their visit. The letter that had brought Bart and Lorraine together again was the very same one that had torn Tate and her apart.

SHE CLOSED KAYLA'S DOOR quietly behind her and walked out into the hall, bypassing her own room in favor of the studio.

Less than twenty-four hours ago she'd been in Tate's arms, her defenses down, her heart ready to try love once again with a man who had a background similar to her own and understood the importance of pursuing a dream. A man who'd held her tenderly, who'd listened to her thoughts and shared his own, who'd made her feel like a woman—desired and appreciated.

But as quickly as he'd come into her life, he had gone. And there was nothing she could do to change it. At least not the part concerning the two of them, anyway. The relationship between Tate and Bart was an entirely different matter.

Phoebe had had to spend holidays alone with her daughter since her grandmother died. Tate didn't. He had a father. A father who truly loved him, yet for many reasons lacked the ability to convey that effectively.

All they needed was a little shove.

She padded on bare feet across the tiny spare bedroom that served as her studio, the moonlight casting shadows across the wooden floor. Her paint jars and brushes were ready and waiting for the next assignment, a job that needed to come soon. Really soon.

Pushing the button on the answering machine, she listened as an unfamiliar voice filled the room.

"Ms. Jennings? My name is April Sumners. I was given your name by my sister, Cara Dolanger."

Phoebe felt her stomach tighten and her palms moisten as the voice continued.

"I saw the portrait you did of Cara and her family, and your work is exquisite. I would like to hire you to do one of my father-in-law, Howard Sumners."

Howard Sumners? The name sounded vaguely familiar.

"He was a professional baseball player in his youth, a driving force in the Red Cross throughout his adulthood. He's getting up in years and we'd like to commission you to capture him…as he is today."

Phoebe shoved aside the mountainous pile of bills on her desk in search of a pen.

"I'd like to set up an appointment with you for this week to talk particulars. I'm anxious to see if you can fit us in."

Fit her in? Was she serious?

"Do you know how many people on that side of town will be tripping over themselves to commission you to paint portraits of their family now? You could rent five buildings."

Tate's words played through her mind, and the urge to call and tell him the news was overpowering. But she couldn't.

Not now. Not ever. He'd made that perfectly clear.

With a long sigh, Phoebe wrote down the woman's number, then crossed to the window, an overwhelming sense of loneliness bubbling up inside. She'd been waiting all her life to make it as an artist. Yet now that it was finally happening, she had no one to share it with—no one who truly understood just how much this dream had always meant to her.

Except one.

Leaning her head against the cool windowpane, she looked out into the moonlit sky.

"I did it, Gram. I really did it," she whispered, and the tears finally began to flow.

Chapter Fourteen

"Welcome back, boss. We've missed you around here the past few days."

Tate looked up from his desk and nodded a greeting at his secretary as she strode across his office, a stack of mail in one hand, a cup of steaming coffee in the other.

"When your partners—ooh, I love how that sounds—told me you were taking a few days off, I nearly fainted. I'd actually convinced myself you didn't understand the concept of vacation." Regina placed the mail in the in-box on the right-hand corner of the desk, the coffee on the coaster to his left. After sweeping her hand in the direction of the mail, she busied herself by checking the few plants in the room. "Most of those are invites to one shindig or another. One, though, is a thank-you note from the Multiple Sclerosis Association for your work on the Innovation House, and another is a résumé from a student in his third year at Ohio State. Young Jake is looking for an opportunity to shadow you for a few weeks."

Tate knew he should be paying attention, getting caught up on everything he'd missed during his self-imposed sulk-athon, but he simply couldn't focus on much of anything. Even something as mundane as invitations and thank-you notes.

"Great. Thanks. I'll take a look." He ran a hand through his hair, then dropped his head into his hands, the area behind his temples beginning to throb.

"Boss?"

He'd thought of little else besides Phoebe over the past three days. Making love with her had been like nothing he'd ever experienced before. And thanks to his temper tantrum on Sunday morning, he wouldn't be experiencing it again anytime soon.

"Boss?"

He was still furious about the letter and the painful realities it had all but confirmed. Yet, in rational moments, he couldn't help but see *another* glaring reality....

Phoebe Jennings hadn't meant any harm by delivering that letter. She'd simply done what any decent person would have.

"Boss!"

Regina's sharp tone made his head snap upward in alarm. "What's wrong?"

"I couldn't have asked it better myself." His secretary marched across the room and poured a glass of water from the pitcher she left on the corner table each morning. Retracing her steps, she divvied the liquid between a potted violet and a fern, put down the glass, then faced him with hands on hips.

"You lost me, Regina."

"That's obvious. Where were you just then?"

He stared at her. "When?"

"Two seconds ago." She pulled a cloth from her

pocket and ran it across the top three shelves along the east wall of his office.

"Uh, right here. In my office. Trying to figure out what you're talking about?"

"No, you weren't. You barely even acknowledged me. You've been off in la-la land since I walked through that door. What gives, boss?"

"Nothing." He picked up his mug and took a long gulp, the liquid searing his throat.

"Then why did you just snip at me *and* do your dandiest to scorch a hole through your neck?"

"I did not snip, and I like my coffee scalding."

She stopped dusting and shook the cloth in the air. "I give up. You're perfectly fine. Next topic."

"Thank you." He waved at the steam rising from his mug before taking another sip.

"I have to tell you... I absolutely adored Phoebe. You've found a real winner in that one, boss."

He thumped his cup on the desk again and leaned his head against the back of his leather chair, the pain in his head intensifying.

"Did I say something wro— Wait! Is *that* the problem? Did something go... What did you *do?*" She sank down in the chair in front of Tate's desk and stared at him, dumbfounded.

If she wasn't so darn perceptive he'd consider protesting her assumption that he'd done something wrong. But it would be an exercise in denial. He knew that as well as she did.

"Not now, Regina."

"Is that why you took the past two days off?"

He arched his eyebrow. "Regina..."

"Okay. Okay. I'll leave you alone." With an air of dejection, she stood and turned on her heel, heading for the door. When she reached her destination she looked over her shoulder, her ultra-efficient-secretary persona fully engaged. "Buzz me if you need something, sir."

As the door closed behind her, he considered calling out, apologizing for his behavior, but he didn't. He simply wasn't ready to talk to *anyone* about the dark cloud pressing down on his heart.

Not even Regina.

Ignoring his mail, Tate spun his chair in a half circle and eyed the latest set of blueprints unfurled across his drafting table. The Cedarville School District had been hemming and hawing over its structural wish list for the new elementary school for months now, adding *this* special lab and *that* state-of-the-art whatever. Yet every time he thought they were finally ready to proceed, they decided to add something different or delete last month's must-have.

Normally, he rolled with the punches, enjoying the opportunity to consider new thoughts and needs. But it was wearing thin.

He was sick of drawings that were, essentially, cookie cutter buildings. There were just so many things you could do with a front entrance and windows.

Designing the Innovation House, however, had been a dream come true. He'd been allowed to follow his imagination, with the only parameters being that there were no parameters at all.

And today was the day the various craftsmen and designers came together to admire the finished project before it was unveiled to the public over the coming

weekend. He'd been looking forward to it for months—
that is, until Sunday. Now, nothing seemed to hold any
allure. Not his clients, not Innovation House and certainly not Cedarville Elementary School.

His office extension rang and was picked up immediately by Regina, who seemed to be handling all calls
in lieu of having to deal with him again. Not that he
could blame her.

He owed her an apology. Spinning around one more
time, he looked at his desk phone and noticed the steady
light beside line two.

As he waited, he grabbed a long slender tube from
beneath his desk and uncapped it, removing an entirely
different set of plans. Slowly, he unrolled the paper and
spread it out across the draft table, his eyes riveted on
the sketch he'd been monkeying around with for a week.
It was a project he hadn't shared with anyone.

He glanced over at the phone, noticed line two was
still lit. *Who on earth?*

Shrugging, he turned back to his sketch, losing himself in assorted tweaks and changes as morning gave
way to the lunch hour.

"Boss?"

He looked from the door to the phone and back again.
"Oh, you're off."

"Off what?" Regina remained in the hallway, her head
the only part of her body visible through the opening.

He pointed at the phone with his pencil. "I wanted
to tell you something, but every time I looked, line two
was lit. Everything okay at home?"

The woman's eyebrows scrunched momentarily.
"Everything's fine. I didn't get any personal ca—" Her

eyebrows suddenly reversed direction and she stepped into his office, still remaining as far from Tate as humanly possible. "What did you need?"

"Why are you standing all the way over there?" He gestured toward the chair across from his desk. "Come, sit. Relax. It's almost lunchtime, right?"

"Will I be beaten?"

"Excuse me?"

"I'm not sure if it's safe to come any closer yet." Regina shifted from foot to foot, a slight grin on her face despite the seriousness she was going for.

"Overstating things just a little, aren't we?"

"No."

He dropped his pencil and stood. "I'm sorry, Regina. I just had a rough weekend and I'm not ready to talk about it yet. When I am, you'll be the first one I come to."

She held up her hands. "No need."

"What?"

"There's no need to tell me."

He stared at her. "Since when? You *always* want to know what's going on."

"I said you didn't need to tell me." She met his eyes with a look that begged to be challenged, and he knew it was best to leave well enough alone. Besides, if he were in her shoes, and she'd been snippy with him when he was only trying to help, he wouldn't care about the source of her mood after a certain point, either.

"Anyway, you better get going or you'll be late." She leaned across the front of his desk and began neatening the area, moving frames and picking up stray paper clips.

"Late for what?"

"The Innovation House event. You *are* going, right?"

"Oh, that." He leaned back in his chair "I don't think so. I'm not really in the mood."

The sound of air being sucked through his secretary's mouth was unmistakable. "But you *have* to," she barked, her cheeks reddening. "I mean…I just mean you worked so hard on that home. You *need* to go. Besides, maybe a change in scenery will be good for you. Help you relax a little."

"Maybe." He glanced down at the plans in front of him, then back up again. "But I've got that meeting I scheduled with the city planning department at three and—"

"It's only noon now. You really need to go. The people from the association expect to meet you."

"Okay, okay. If you really think I should."

"Off you go. *Now.*"

"Is there a fire I don't know about?" he asked as he reached for his suit jacket.

"I…I just don't want you to be late. This is a big deal, you know? I don't want one of the other partners to come in here and start jabbering so much you miss it completely."

His partners *jabbered?* That wasn't a verb he'd use in conjunction with either one of them, but he let it go. Regina was right. He needed to attend. If for no other reason than to be a team player—for a worthy cause.

TATE WALKED THROUGH the first floor in awe. He'd known what Innovation House was going to look like— he'd designed it himself. He'd even seen various stages during the construction phase, consulting about his blueprints when needed. But to walk through it as a completed home was like nothing he could have imagined.

Each room had been decorated by one of a half dozen interior designers in the area, professionals who had donated their services and products for the chance to help a charity and gain the attention of both the media and potential customers.

Tate had taken a gamble by going with twelve-foot ceilings on the first floor, but it had paid off. Any worry over the size impacting a homey feel was eliminated as he walked through the library, with its mahogany shelves, roll-along ladder, old-fashioned chandelier and cozy armchairs. The kitchen, a larger version of his own, simply offered more space for enjoying a family meal.

Slowly, he climbed the stairs to the second floor and walked through each and every bedroom. The wall-mounted mirror that did double duty as a flat-screen television was a touch he'd never seen in a master bedroom before. The his and her closets off the master bath were state-of-the-art, with revolving shelves, hidden bays and permanent cedar storage. The children's playroom was one of his favorite spaces in the whole house, thanks to the built-in loft beds to accommodate sleepovers and a raised area that could serve as a stage for make-believe shows.

Along the way he shook hands with various decorators, artists and construction workers. And couldn't help but wish Phoebe was here to see it. In fact, Innovation House would be a fantastic place to showcase her portraits.

"She'd be booked a year ahead if her work was in here…" His voice trailed off as he realized he'd spoke aloud. Looking around, he shrugged away the questioning glance from a decorative painter he barely knew, before making a beeline for the third floor.

Unlike its wooden counterpart between the first and second floors, the staircase leading to the third floor was covered in the plushest of carpets, his feet leaving indents with each step he took. Rounding the newel post at the top, he slowed his pace to allow a disabled woman and her husband to exit the elevator into the rec room.

When he'd first drawn the elevator, Tate had considered removing it again for the simple fact that few private residences had one. But when he considered the foundation's "anything goes" attitude, he'd left it alone.

Now, knowing it could provide individuals access to a room they might not normally be able to enjoy, he realized he'd made a good decision.

He watched with admiration as the woman advanced, carrying herself with poise despite the cane in her hand. Her husband, smartly dressed in khaki slacks and a white polo, walked beside her, his hand gently placed against her lower back. They were a neat couple, Tate decided.

"Why don't you go ahead? I don't want to slow you down." The woman, clad in a simple summer dress, pushed a piece of graying hair from her face and smiled at him.

"No. Please. I'm not in any rush." Tate gestured for them to go ahead, his gaze moving from the woman's face to her husba—

"Young man, are you okay?"

He knew the woman was speaking, sensed her mouth moving and her eyes widening with worry. But he couldn't focus on anything except the man staring back at him.

"Hello, Tate."

He swallowed, an effort made difficult by the tightening in his throat and the thumping of his heart. "Dad."

"Tate? This is your son?" The woman stepped forward and embraced him with her right arm, seemingly unaware of the way Tate's body tensed at her touch. "I had no idea you were going to be here. How wonderful."

"That's not the word I'd use," he finally said.

"Lorraine, why don't you go ahead and tour this floor on your own? I'll meet you downstairs later. My son and I need to talk."

"I have nothing to say," Tate snapped.

"Then you can listen."

He watched as his father kissed the woman on her cheek and then motioned for Tate to follow him to the fourth-floor deck. "It might not be the most private of places, but at least we'll have some fresh air," his dad stated.

"I'd prefer a stiff drink," Tate muttered. Yet, for some unknown reason, he felt his feet taking charge and following his father up the steps and onto the deck. He'd been looking forward to seeing the top floor ever since he'd stepped through the front door, anxious to check out the private hot tub space he'd included in the plans. But now that he was there, he couldn't care less.

"There are some things I need to say to you. Things I wish I'd explained years and years ago, but didn't." His father leaned his forearms on the railing that encased the entire fourth floor. "We never should have allowed ourselves to disappear from each other's lives when your mom passed away. She'd be devastated if she knew, and she deserves better."

"Deserves better? *Deserves better?*" Tate felt his

hands beginning to shake, so he balled them into fists at his sides. "You're a fine one to talk about Mom deserving better."

"You couldn't be more right."

He stared at his father in confusion. "What?"

"Your mother was a beautiful, warm, loving human being who, for whatever reason, saw something in me worth loving even when I didn't."

Huh?

Tate shook his head, trying to keep up with everything he was saying.

"When your mother came into my life I was in bad shape. I'd been hurt, deeply, and felt nothing mattered anymore. Most women of your mom's caliber would have taken one look at me and run for the hills. But she didn't. She saw something even *I* couldn't see.

"Slowly, with her help, I began to wake up, to see the possibility of a better tomorrow. I warned her that I was gun-shy, even bitter, but she didn't care." The elder Williams raised a trembling hand to his face and brushed at a tear that had escaped his left eye. "We married and eventually had you. My life was as perfect as I could imagine it being, and I was terrified it was going to slip through my fingers, or, even worse, blow up in my face."

Tate hung on every word the man said, afraid that if he breathed too loudly he'd miss something.

"So I held a part of my heart back. As a defense mechanism."

"Why?" It was all Tate could think to ask, but it was sufficient.

He listened closely as his father explained his history

with Lorraine Walters. Tate asked occasional questions as they popped into his mind, and found the tale made sense, to a point.

"But why couldn't you just love Mom and me the way we loved you?"

Tear-filled eyes turned to look at him. "I *did.* I was just terrified to show it. I'd watched my own father go out for milk one afternoon, only to never come home again. I poured my heart out to Lorraine, and never got a response. I guess I saw love as a recipe for hurt. So while I did love deeply inside, I was afraid to let down my guard and show it."

Tate leaned against the railing beside his father. "Did mom know you were still hung up on this other woman?"

"Not 'hung up on.' Hurt by. And I think your mother understood more about me than even *I* did."

It fit. And Tate told his father so. "She looked at you with pure love until the day she died. That's what hurt me so much. She was so amazing, so loving, so *in love* with you, yet you seemed to take it all for granted."

"Not for granted, son. Never for granted. It was quite the opposite…. I was paralyzed at the thought of ever relaxing enough to trust in that love."

Tate closed his eyes as another question came to him, one his mind was itching to ask, while his heart dreaded the answer. Finally, though, he murmured, "Do you still love Lorraine?"

His father straightened up and took a step closer. "Still? No. I still love your mother. As for Lorraine, I think the more accurate thing to say is that I love her again."

It was a simple statement, but a heartfelt one, and it

made all the difference in the world to Tate. He reached out, cupped his father's shoulder gently. "Thank you. For making me listen."

Tate leaned his back against the railing and looked around. "Pretty nice, huh?"

"Nice? I think I'd say *spectacular*. You are a fine architect, son. I'm proud of you."

A familiar stinging began behind his eyes, a sensation he'd experienced just three days earlier. Only that time it was out of anger—at himself.

Pride was definitely better.

For several long minutes they simply stood there, each lost in his own thoughts. Finally, Tate swallowed and in a husky voice admitted, "I never thought you cared what I did."

"Of course I cared. I just didn't much understand the drawing and that whole artistic bond you and your mother shared. To learn about it would have forced me to get closer. But I *did* care. In fact, I still have the very first architectural sketch you ever drew in my apartment. Under glass, so it's protected."

Tate stared at him. "You do?"

"I do. It was a tree house you and Johnny Haskell were determined to build."

He swallowed again over the lump in his throat, which seemed to be growing tighter the longer they talked. "I heard what you did with the Quinton Lane crowd. How you tried to make them understand that the whole Les Walker thing was out of my hands."

His father's brows furrowed. "How'd you hear that?"

"It doesn't matter. I just know."

Tate smiled as his dad cleared his throat awkwardly,

then quickly changed the subject. "Lorraine said this home is going to make a lot of money for MS."

"Is that why you're here?" he asked, as pieces began to fall into place. "Is that why she uses a cane?"

"She works for the charity the money is going to, and yes, she suffers from the disease, as well. But she's doing remarkably well. She always was a strong woman."

"Think you'll propose again?"

He felt his father's eyes studying him. "You don't think that would be too fast? It's only been a week."

Tate laughed. "A week plus forty years."

"That's the kind of cut-to-the-chase your mother would have employed." Bart Williams smiled despite the sadness in his eyes. "I miss her, Tate. Every single day."

"As do I." He pushed himself off the railing, took three strides forward, then turned around and came back. "Life is too short to live in the past—that's there for the memories. Life is about living. It's about today and tomorrow…"

A blanket of silence fell between them as a group of people walked around the outer ring of the deck and then headed back toward the stairs.

"That was beautiful, son."

"It was spoken by a beautiful woman. And she's right. The past is gone, over. The only chance for change and growth is in the future."

"Sounds like you have your own special someone."

"Had someone special. I blew it."

"Do you love her, son?"

The answer came easily. "Yes. Very much."

Tate felt his father's hand on his shoulder. "Then stop pushing and start pulling."

"I'm not sure I deserve her." He swallowed yet again. "She's beautiful and generous and kind and loving and...I can't even begin to do her justice."

"Sounds an awful lot like your mom."

Without thinking, Tate pulled his father into an embrace and simply held him, seconds melting into minutes. When they finally released one another and stepped back, he looked out over West Cedarville, his thoughts centered on a very different side of town.

"Do you know what the hardest part of forgiveness is, son?"

Tate shook his head, too choked with feelings to utter any words.

"Being able to forgive *yourself.*"

Chapter Fifteen

If she'd known how hectic her week was going to be, Phoebe would have politely declined Bart's invitation for dinner. Time with Kayla had been at a premium of late and she needed the cuddles and kisses more than polite conversation.

But she'd agreed to be there and didn't believe in backing out of a commitment for anything short of an emergency. And, last she checked, a broken heart and mommy time didn't qualify.

Glancing at her wristwatch, Phoebe knocked on Bart's door and waited, mentally calculating the minimal amount of time she could stay before excusing herself for the night. Sure, she was happy for Bart and Lorraine, and pleased they wanted her to be a part of their celebration, but she was finding it harder and harder to hide her relationship-gone-wrong with his son.

"Phoebe, you're here!" Bart stepped into the hallway and embraced her, a wide smile on his face. "Lorraine will be along soon. She is so anxious to finally meet you."

"That makes two of us then," Phoebe said as she

followed him into his apartment. And it was true. She was excited to meet the woman who'd written a letter that had changed so many lives, not the least of which was Phoebe's own.

"We couldn't imagine anyone we'd rather share our happiness with than the two of you."

"Two?" She stopped and turned toward Bart, waiting as he shut the door. He led her to the kitchen area, where the aroma of tomatoes and garlic permeated the air, and her stomach grumbled in response.

"Two." Bart gestured for her to follow as he headed into the living room. "Not only did your letter bring Lorraine and me together, it also gave my son and me the kick we needed to move forward."

She grabbed the back edge of the sofa to steady herself, Bart's words taking root at the same time she heard a knock. "Your *son?*"

Nodding, he stepped back toward the door. "Yes, my son. Lorraine and I ran into him at Innovation House on Wednesday and we had a long overdue talk. I've got a lot of time to try and make up to him, but he seems willing to give me the chance."

In any other setting she'd have been thrilled at the news, pleased that her phone call to Regina had put father and son in the same place at the same time. Unfortunately, standing in the middle of Bart's living room, with Tate due any minute, wasn't one of those settings.

The last time they'd seen each other had been in her front hallway, with his face contorted in anger. At her. She was the last person Tate Williams would want to see when he walked through the door.

"Bart?" She fell into step with him as he made his

way through the kitchen, her stomach no longer interested in dinner. "I don't think I should stay."

He stopped, his eyes widening in surprise. "Why on earth not?"

"Because this is an evening you and your son should have alone with Lorraine. I just delivered a letter. That's all." Phoebe clasped her hands, hoping that would stop them trembling.

"That's *all?*" Bart started walking again. "That's a pretty big thing if you ask me. Especially considering that without that letter Lorraine and I never would have met and I wouldn't have been at Innovation House to see my son again."

She tried another tactic. "Mending fences can take a while. You don't need a stranger horning in on that time."

Bart stopped once again. "My son said something to me the other day that sums this up. He said life is about living. The past is about memories, the present and future is for living."

"He said *that?*" She felt her jaw drop as she tried to absorb what she was hearing.

"He sure did. Though, in all fairness, he worded it more eloquently. Said he heard it from a beautiful woman." Reaching for the doorknob, Bart glanced over his shoulder. "Sad part is he's in love with her, but says he's blown it."

"In love—" She did a combination gasp and choke.

Nodding, he pulled the door open. "I hope, for his sake, it works out. He's a good kid—always was. I'm just sorry he didn't meet you first."

TATE FELT HIS MUSCLES tensing at the sound of Phoebe's voice. He'd begun second-guessing himself about the surprise meeting earlier in the day, his apprehension only increasing as dinner drew closer. For all he knew, she would take one look at him and bolt. Or worse yet, scream at him the way he deserved.

But as the door opened, he realized none of that mattered. He was willing to take his chances just to have an opportunity to see her again. To try to make amends. Somehow.

"Hello, son. It's great to see you again."

Tate tried to look at his dad, to match his enthusiastic greeting, but all he could focus on was the woman standing beside him, her eyes cast downward, her expression uncertain. Still looking at Phoebe, he stuck out a hand to his father. "Hi. It's great to be here."

His heart threatened to stop as she slowly raised her head, her khaki-green eyes peering out from behind long, black lashes. It didn't matter how many times he saw her, she still took his breath away each and every time.

"Tate, I'd like you to meet my very special friend, Phoebe Jennings." His father turned to her and gestured. "Phoebe, this is my son, Tate."

Tate stepped into the apartment just as a voice from the corridor claimed his father's attention.

"Lorraine!"

Seizing the momentary reprieve while his father was busy, Tate edged closer to Phoebe, searching for any indication she might be happy to see him. What he detected in her face, though, was wariness.

"H-hi," she stammered. "I'm so sorry, I had absolutely no idea you were going to be here."

"No worries, please." He started to move closer, then

stopped. "It's good you're here. *Great,* actually." He studied her for a long moment. "You look tired."

She shrugged. "I've been busy. The phone has been ringing off the hook with job offers. I guess the Dolangers know more people than I realized."

"I think it's more a matter of your talent being enjoyed by hundreds on a daily basis."

"Hundreds?"

"Last I heard that's about how many folks were visiting the Innovation House each day. It's amazing."

"Yeah, but I don't have anything there…"

As her eyes widened with realization, it was his turn to shrug. "Look, the suggestion may have gotten it on the wall…but it's your talent, and your talent alone, that's drumming up the business. Don't forget that."

They were interrupted by Lorraine's entry into the apartment and the lengthy introduction that followed.

"Let's head into the living room and let the women chat." Tate felt his father's hand on his upper back, a touch he actually welcomed. "In the meantime, I want to talk to you about those plans."

Tate felt his stomach twist as they followed the two through the kitchen and into the sitting area. There were so many things he wanted to say to Phoebe, to explain about himself and his past, but the timing was off. Especially considering his father was still in the dark about their relationship.

Or what had been blooming into a relationship prior to temper tantrum number three.

His father guided him toward the small rolltop desk, and Tate tried to concentrate on the sketch that was being unfurled. But it was darn near impossible when all he wanted to do was to grab Phoebe by the hand and beg for one last chance.

"I think this—" his father gestured to the drawing of a gazebo and walkway "—should satisfy the committee. It's attractive, usable and quaint."

"I actually presented it to them a few days ago. They loved it, so it's a go." He took a deep breath as he looked at the sketch he'd given his father after their first meeting. "Now, if I can call in a favor from one of my construction buddies, maybe we can get the labor for free, too."

Tate shot a glance in Phoebe's direction, but her back was to him as she conversed with Lorraine. As much as the juvenile side of him wanted to dislike his father's girlfriend, he couldn't. In fact, after getting a chance to know her at Innovation House, after he and his father had talked, he had to admit he understood why his dad was so smitten.

She was a sweet woman.

"Let me make a few calls myself and see what I can do in terms of getting stuff donated," Bart said.

"You don't have to do that."

"I want to. Quinton Lane was special to me, too. It's where I spent the happiest years of my life, with the two people I loved most in the world."

Tate found himself getting choked up. The doubt he'd harbored as to his father's feelings about his mother were dissipating. Bart Williams may have had issues with rejection and trust, but he *had* loved his wife—a simple fact that made their son feel happier and more at peace.

"Thank you, Dad. I want the green space to be there for Kayla just as it was for me."

Bart's head shot up and he grinned. "What do you know? Phoebe has a baby named Kayla."

At the sound of her daughter's name, Phoebe looked over her shoulder at Tate, giving him the boost he needed to admit everything.

"I know that, Dad."

Bart looked confused. "You do?"

He nodded, his gaze never leaving Phoebe's face. In just a few short weeks he'd fallen in love with the woman—head over heels in love. Seeing her so close, yet knowing they were so far apart, was ripping his heart in two and he was determined to fix that once and for all.

"Remember that woman I told you about, the one who told me to stop looking backward? To concentrate instead on today and tomorrow? Well, she's sitting right there, looking at both of us. She's beautiful, smart, talented, loving, funny, gentle, caring and so much more. But I took my frustration and my unwillingness to forgive you out on her. And I did it in a cruel way and with horrendous timing."

His heart ached to hold Phoebe as she stood to face him.

"The moment I saw Phoebe standing in my doorway with your letter in her hand, I felt something. When she left, I thought of little else, imagined seeing her again one day." He took a step toward her, and their eyes locked. "And, miraculously, I did see her again. And again. And again. She's in my thoughts constantly when we're not together, an affliction that's only gotten worse."

He took a deep breath. "I asked her to forgive me once, twice, for my atrocious behavior, and she did. Now I'm hoping she'll give me one more chance, because I'm confident she won't regret it. Ever. I'll do everything in my power to make sure of that."

This time Phoebe took a step in his direction. "I could never regret a decision that makes me feel as if I'm floating on air and ready to face a new day," she said with a smile.

"Does that mean what I think it means?" Tate closed the remaining distance between them.

"Son, I may have been a bit too much of an observer at times, but I know I taught you to use your brains." Bart walked around the sofa and pulled Lorraine to her feet, lovingly placing her cane in her hand. "As for us, I have an uncanny knack for knowing when sauce needs to be stirred. So I'll get right to it."

Tate looked at Phoebe, then rolled his eyes upward. "Could you walk a little faster, Dad?"

"I'm going, I'm going." The elderly man looped an arm over Lorraine's shoulders, then glanced back at Phoebe and winked. "He's a tad pushy at times, but he's a keeper."

"I know," she whispered as Tate pulled her into his arms, seeking her lips with his own.

Chapter Sixteen

"What do you hear?"

Phoebe felt Tate's hand on her shoulder, halting her movement. "Um—voices."

"Very good. Can you pick any of them out?"

Tilting her head slightly, she listened for the various inflections and tones she'd come to know over the past six months. "I hear Ms. Weatherby...oh, and Mr. Haskell." She craned her head forward, trying to discern a set of voices that seemed to be coming from somewhere ahead. "Mr. Borden?"

"Anyone ever tell you you have eagle ears?"

Phoebe grinned and swiveled her head to the side. "No, but someone recently told me I have amazing lips."

A warm sensation rippled against her ear. "Among other things. *Lots* of other things."

"You did mention a time or two...something about my bacon-cooking ability. Is that one of the things you're referring to?"

The warmth along her ear was quickly replaced by a tingle of desire through her entire body. "Not quite."

"You're holding out on me, mister." She tried to bat

her eyelashes, but realized it was futile. Bandannas had a way of hiding such effects.

"Technically, yes. But only because my dad and Lorraine are about ten steps ahead of us, and if I participate in this verbal volley any more than I already am, we're not going to make this shindig."

"I'm good with that."

Tate's laugh resonated through the air as his hands began fumbling with the knot he'd made at the back of her head. "I would be, too, except everyone is kind of looking at you right now."

She jerked in surprise. "Looking at me? Why?"

"They want to see what you think of—this!"

With one final tug, he pulled the cloth from her eyes and she blinked against the bright afternoon sun. Sure enough, standing a half dozen yards away were her Quinton Lane neighbors, gathered at the edge of the green space to celebrate their victory against the city.

A victory she'd been unaware of until twenty minutes ago, when Tate had decided to break his silence.

Slowly, she took in the field that had been the setting for parties and celebrations among her neighbors since long before she and Kayla had moved onto the street. A line of new trees had been planted, set off to the side to provide shade over the years, while keeping the open space.

"Where did *that* come from?" She pointed to the walking path that meandered off among the trees.

"Don't you mean, where does it go?" A mischievous grin spread across Tate's face.

"Bart?"

The elder Williams stepped toward her, Kayla in his arms. "Yes?"

"Was he always this way?"

The man's gaze swept his son, then he shrugged. "He was always good at those games where you wait to see who gives in first. Drove Johnny Haskell nuts."

Again Tate laughed, a sound so rich and so genuine it made Phoebe's heart race and her knees grow weak. "Okay, okay, let's follow it."

Kayla squealed.

"You met with *her* approval." Tate waved at Kayla, then grasped Phoebe's hand. "I think she's excited to see your reaction, too."

Never in her wildest imagination could she have dreamed up a man like Tate Williams. For herself or her daughter.

"Has she seen it?" She squeezed his fingers and began walking along the path, a cluster of neighbors in front, a cluster behind.

"Every step of the way."

Phoebe frowned as she thought back over the two weeks since the dinner at Bart's. "When?"

"Every night. When I encouraged you to take a little more time to paint."

"Is *this* where you two disappeared to?"

"Well—most of the time." Tate picked up speed as they walked along a curved stretch of pathway. "Sometimes we got waylaid. You wouldn't believe how many cookies your daughter can get simply by flashing that smile of hers."

Phoebe laughed. "Trust me, I know. And don't think she isn't learning to work it."

"Nah, I think she's just got that special something her mom has—so beautifully rare that few people are lucky enough to be blessed with it." He stopped and turned to her, suddenly looking more serious than he had all morning. "Will you shut your eyes for a few more steps? So we can really surprise you?"

"Okay." She pinched her eyes shut, her body warming as Tate's hand left hers and his arm wrapped around her back. Slowly, step by step, she walked, the only sounds she heard belonging to a few birds and her own daughter.

When she felt his hand tighten against her back she stopped. Waited.

"Ready, everyone?"

"Let her go, Tate."

She recognized Mr. Borden's voice as Tate's mouth moved against her ear once again. "On a count of three, everyone…"

"One…"

That had to be Mrs. Haskell. Her singsong voice always reminded Phoebe of a favorite elementary-school teacher when she and Gram had lived in Paulson.

"Two."

Ms. Weatherby. Everything she said had a slightly biting snap to it, as if she were in a hurry all the time. Not because she was impatient, but simply on the go.

"Eeee."

Phoebe's eyes flew open as Kayla's voice, sweet and proud, reached her ears.

"Good job, sweet—"

Her jaw dropped as her eyes took in the white trellised gazebo just beyond her daughter's head. The outdoor structure, typical of small towns and civic greens, stood proudly on the other side of the walkway, beckoning to them.

"How? When? Oh, Tate, it's beautiful." She turned her head to the handsome man beside her, neatly clad in khaki pants and a blue button-down shirt. A man who had learned to put aside hurt in order to move forward.

One by one, her neighbors began to clap, their focus not on her, but on Tate. She watched as his face turned red and a look of pride lit his eyes.

"Don't my flowers look lovely around the base? Really brings the gazebo to life." Mrs. Applewhite smiled grandly at her neighbors before turning to beam at Tate.

"You're right, Mrs. Applewhite, they do. I'm betting they made all the difference with the city planning board."

Phoebe looked up at Tate, in awe over his excitement and the fact he showed absolutely no signs of being deterred by a woman who wasn't happy unless she was ahead.

"You saved our green space, young man, and we…" Mr. Borden cleared his throat and shot an authoritative look in Mrs. Applewhite's direction before turning back to Tate "…are forever grateful to you."

Tate shifted a bit awkwardly, his arm still around Phoebe's back. "It's my pleasure. I'm finally at a place in my career where I could call in a few favors. Dad did, too. This place meant a lot to both of us and holds some of my fondest memories of my mother."

Phoebe felt his eyes on her just before he pulled her closer. "But now it's time to make new memories. For all of us." He released her and held out his hands to Kayla, who squealed in delight and raised her arms in response. "Can't you just see this little angel having tea parties in there?" He pointed toward the gazebo. "Or one of Mr. Haskell's famed fall barbecue dinners at those picnic tables? I know I sure can."

Heads bobbed in agreement.

"Okay. So let's get to making some of those new memories." The words were no sooner out of his mouth than the Quinton Lane crowd took off toward the gazebo, their steps propelled by the promise of a potluck dinner.

Phoebe and Tate lingered behind with Kayla.

"I'm sorry about Mrs. Applewhite just now. She really is a thunder stealer."

He shrugged. "Only if we let her steal it."

Phoebe cocked an eyebrow and waited.

"Mrs. Applewhite was always competitive, for as long as I can remember. But she was especially bad where my mom was concerned."

"Mr. Borden said the same thing."

Phoebe felt Tate's arm slide around her waist again, his breath on her ear. "See those purple flowers right there? To the left of the gazebo steps?"

"Ahh, yes."

"Look just above them," he whispered. "On the base itself."

Squinting against the sun, she noticed a flash of something golden. "You mean that gold-colored rectangle?"

He nodded, a smile lighting his face with a mixture of pride and monkey business. "It's a plaque. The Quinton Lane gazebo was designed and built in honor of my mother. And, unlike flowers, it's a memento that will be there no matter the season."

"Perfect!"

And it was. Everyone who spoke of Mary Williams had adored her. Therefore it seemed only fitting she'd have a part in the green space's new beginning. But still...

"I can't believe you did all this. The planning. The execution. It's extraordinary."

He pointed at his chest. "You doubt my architectural skills?"

"Hardly." She ran her finger along his jawline, across his lips and up toward his hair, wishing they were alone together. "I just meant your doing this after— Well, you know."

He shrugged. "They made a mistake. They've apologized. Some of those cookies—" he moved his finger back and forth between himself and Kayla "—we scored during our walks were for me, too, you know."

"Ook!" the toddler squealed.

"Uh-oh, now you did it. There's no mentioning that word around my daughter unless you can produce." Phoebe tickled her gently under the chin and laughed when she giggled.

"Hold on now," Tate proclaimed as they fell into step. "I hate to break it to you, but Kayla's face wasn't the only one that lit up just now at the mention of a cookie."

"I *know*. But how did you see it?" Phoebe glanced around, peeking behind the last of the trees. "There isn't a mirror anywhere."

He looked at Kayla and blinked his eyes angelically. "Is Mommy calling *me* a cookie monster?"

"Ook!"

Smacking his head with the heel of his hand, Tate grunted. "I walked into that one, didn't I?"

"Yup."

"Well then, if you'll excuse us, we have some cookies to find." Tate cupped Phoebe's head with his hand and pulled her toward him for a fast but heart-melting kiss. "I love you, Phoebe Jennings."

She blinked back the sudden moisture in her eyes as she watched Tate and Kayla enter the gazebo, her neighbors turning to greet them with smiles of appreciation and affection.

"Oh, Gram," Phoebe whispered, "you were right. The best was yet to come."

TATE SCOOTED ACROSS the blanket and wrapped his arm around Phoebe's waist, careful not to nudge a sleeping Kayla. An afternoon of play and cookies had taken its toll on the littlest Jennings.

"Having a good time?" he asked softly.

"The best." Phoebe reached down and mussed his hair, her touch sending a warm feeling of contentment through him.

"Me, too." He jerked his head to the left. "Dad sure looks happy, doesn't he?"

Phoebe followed his gaze, then nodded. "He does. Are you really okay with him and Lorraine getting married?"

Tate watched as his father leaned across his own picnic blanket and handed a daylily to his special lady, a look of bliss on his face. "A month ago, I'd have been furious. Convinced it was a betrayal of my mother."

"And now?" Phoebe prodded.

"I know Mom would want him to be happy. She loved him. Completely. Unconditionally. The way it's supposed to be." Tate sat up, gently caressing Phoebe's cheek. "The way he loved her in return. And the way I love you."

He saw the sudden glistening in her eyes, knew it mirrored his own. Grabbing her hand, he pulled it to his mouth and kissed each finger gently. "What would you think of making Dad and Lorraine's wedding a double ceremony?"

As Phoebe's mouth began to open, he moved in for a kiss, the feel of her lips against his solidifying everything he knew to be true.

"What are you talking about?"

His voice rough with emotion, he answered, "It seems only fitting that we marry alongside the other couple brought together by that letter."

"We?"

In a flash he was on his knees, her hand in his, their eyes locked. "Will you marry me, Phoebe Jennings?"

"I—I—I."

Tate peeked around Phoebe's shoulder and grinned at the little girl who'd just opened her eyes, a smile lighting her face.

"I got it!" Waving away Phoebe's giggle, he continued, "That time it meant yes."

At the sight of Phoebe's head shaking, he felt his shoulders droop. "It doesn't?"

"No. That was a hi."

"Oh."

"This is a yes—Tate Williams, I'd love to be your wife."

"Really?"

"Absolutely."

"Are you sure? You threw me off a little when you asked if I thought it was too soon for Dad and Lorraine."

"We may have known each other only a month, but I've been looking for you my whole life."

She sank into his arms, his tears mingling with hers as they held each other close.

Epilogue

Thirteen Months Later

Phoebe waddled slowly down Quinton Lane, the manila envelope tucked securely under her arm as an unseasonably warm breeze kicked up around her, causing more than a few autumn leaves to skitter across the sidewalk.

"How are you this morning, Phoebe?"

She stopped beside Ms. Weatherby's freshly painted, waist-high picket fence and took a few breaths. "I'm good. Tired, but good."

"You make sure you're soaking those feet from time to time. And let that husband of yours baby you a little." The street's lone centurion leaned across the fence and wiggled her finger at Phoebe. "I've not seen a man try so hard to take care of a woman before."

And she was right. Tate was attentive with a capital A. To both her *and* Kayla.

"Speaking of my husband, he and Kayla were nowhere to be found when I woke up. His car is on the street, so I know he didn't go far. Have you seen him?"

The woman, whose body was becoming more frail with each passing day, slowly nodded. "I did. Those two peas in a pod are over at Tom Borden's house. And I tell you, there's been a lot of noise coming from that workshop he's got out back. Building something, no doubt, just like the old days."

Phoebe smiled. "Thanks, Ms. Weatherby. I'm going to see if I can find them now. I'll stop back on the way home, see if you need anything."

"A nap. That's all I need. Not much you can do to help me with that except get those men to stop hammering for a while."

"I'll give it a shot." She touched her hand and gave it a gentle squeeze. "Thank you."

"Give my love to Tate and Kayla, will you?"

"I will."

As she continued on her path, she couldn't help but marvel at how Tate and their neighbors had moved past old wounds as if they'd never happened. Now, instead of avoiding the subject of Quinton Lane, Tate was out and about whenever he had a spare moment, helping their various neighbors with whatever project needed to be done. Even Mrs. Applewhite.

Phoebe turned up Mr. Borden's walkway and knocked on the door, and soon the sound of his walker reached her through the open screen.

"Hi there, Phoebe. What a nice surprise!" He pushed the screen door open and scooted his walker to the right. "Come in, come in."

She stepped into the foyer, wincing at a quick jab of pain in her abdomen. When it subsided, she inhaled slowly, aware of her neighbor's eyes trained on hers.

"They're out on the sunporch. Setting up my old train track."

"*Your* train track? How'd you manage that? Last I saw it you'd just sold it to a very nice young man from a few streets over."

Mr. Borden pushed his walker down the hall and into the breakfast room. "Well, I remember how much Tate had loved my trains when he was growing up, and I simply couldn't let them go."

"So, how'd you get it back?"

"I'll tell you this much…" the man lowered his voice and looked around, as if someone might be listening "…that kid drives one helluva bargain. Not only would he not sell them to me for the price he paid, he also charged me an extra ten cents."

"You've taught him well, then." She pulled the envelope from under her arm and looked down at the broken seal, her smile growing ever wider at the knowledge of what was inside.

"Could you spare Tate for just a moment? I need to give him this." She held up the envelope, then brought it back down to her side.

"Of course." He gripped the top bars of his walker and pushed it toward the sunroom. "I'll hang out with Kayla for a little while and send Tate out to you."

"Thank you." As she waited, she tapped the manila envelope against her leg and Mr. Borden's wall. She would have preferred Tate had been home with her when it was delivered, but either way, he was going to be thrilled—no matter where he read the letter.

"Hey, beautiful, why aren't you home resting?" Tate

strode down the hallway toward her, stopping to plant a kiss on her lips and hold her close.

"A letter came for you."

One eyebrow shot up. "A letter? Is it an old one?"

She looked up at him from the safety of his arms and grinned. "It's got a current postmark…it's just been a long time coming."

"Wait, is that—" He snatched the envelope from her outstretched hand and opened it. "It is!"

"It's official. You are legally Kayla's daddy."

"Kayla's daddy!" he repeated, a joyful smile tugging at his lips. "You know, I like all these titles I get from being with you."

"Titles?" She rubbed her belly, wincing as another pain shot through her.

"Yeah. Kayla's daddy…Phoebe's husband…it's incredible." He pulled her closer and whispered in her ear, "Come on out into the sunroom. Kayla and I have something to show you."

The pain gone once again, she followed her husband down the hall toward the sound of happy chattering. "Hi, sweetie."

"Hi, Mommy. Look what Daddy did." She pointed at the train set in the middle of the room and clapped excitedly. "I did the houses."

"And you did a very good job." Phoebe lowered herself onto the wicker sofa that had been pushed to the side of the room to accommodate the train set, mustering a smile as a way to placate the worry she noticed in Mr. Borden's eyes.

"Look what I found in your old shed, Tom." Bart Williams burst through the door leading from the backyard just then. "Conductor hats. One for Tate and one for Kayla." He leaned over, plopped one hat on his granddaughter's head and tossed one to his son. "Try it on, see if it fits—oh, hi, Phoebe. Didn't see you sitting there."

"Hi yourself."

"Hey, Phoebe, look at us."

She swung her gaze from Bart to Tate, her heart bursting with love at the sight of Kayla in her husband's arms, the inseparable duo sporting matching blue-and-white engineer hats.

"Okay, Kayla, go," he prompted.

The little girl's right hand shot into the air, pulling downward in a deliberate motion. "Woo-woo! All ba-board!"

Tate's eyes twinkled with pride as he squeezed Kayla tight before looking over at Phoebe. "So, Mommy, where should we go on Kayla's train?"

"Oh!" A pain, not unlike the other two, shot through her stomach, nearly launching her to her feet.

"'Oh'? We don't know where *that* is, do we, Kayla?" He jiggled the little girl on his forearm, laughing at her squeals. "Try again, Mommy."

Phoebe held her breath as the pain slowly subsided, enabling her to string a sentence together. "I'd go anywhere so long as I could be with the two of you...but we need to make a delivery first."

"What, now?" Tate asked, getting to his feet.

Pushing herself up from the chair, she slid a hand to her stomach. "Don't you mean *who?*"

"Nooo." Tate's eyebrows dipped as he looked at her, confusion replacing the playful sparkle in his eyes.

Bart crossed his arms in front of his chest and shook his head. "Son. You're smarter than this."

"What?" Tate set Kayla down on the ground and held his hands up, palms out. "I don't have a clue what either of you are talking about…." Confusion gave way to understanding before getting booted away by an entirely different sparkle. "It's time?"

"Yep."

Tate raised his arms into the air in victory, then lunged forward, sliding his arm around Phoebe's waist and guiding her toward the door. They'd made it about three feet when he stopped to look over his shoulder, his breath warm against her ear. "Dad? Mr. Borden?"

"We'll take good care of her, son, don't you worry."

"Thanks, Dad."

They made it a few steps closer to the door when Tate stopped once again. This time, she felt his palms on her shoulders, turning her to face him. "I love you, Phoebe Jennings."

"Oh! Oh!" She gripped her stomach with one hand, his arm with the other.

"I'll take that as a ditto."

*Fan favorite Leslie Kelly is bringing her readers
a fantasy so scandalous, we're calling it FORBIDDEN!*

Look for
PLAY WITH ME

Available February 2010 from Harlequin® Blaze™

"AREN'T YOU GOING to say 'Fly me' or at least
'Welcome aboard'?"

Amanda Bauer didn't. The softly muttered word
that actually came out of her mouth was a lot less
welcoming. And had fewer letters. Four, to be exact.

The man shook his head and tsked. "Not exactly
the friendly skies. Haven't caught the spirit yet this
morning?"

"Make one more airline-slogan crack and you'll be
walking to Chicago," she said.

He nodded once, then pushed his sunglasses onto the
top of his tousled hair. The move revealed blue eyes that
matched the sky above. And yeah. They were twinkling.
Damn it.

"Understood. Just, uh, promise me you'll say 'Coffee,
tea or me' at least once, okay? Please?"

Amanda tried to glare, but that twinkle sucked the
annoyance right out of her.

Coffee and tea they had, and he was welcome to
them. But her? Well, she'd never even considered
making a move on a customer before. Talk about
unprofessional.

And yet...

Something inside her suddenly wanted to take a
chance, to be a little outrageous.

How long since she had done indecent things—or

decent ones, for that matter—with a sexy man? She hadn't had time for a lunch date, much less the kind of lust-fest she'd enjoyed in her younger years. The kind that lasted for entire weekends and involved not leaving a bed except to grab the kind of sensuous food that could be smeared onto—and eaten off—someone else's hot, naked, sweat-tinged body.

She closed her eyes, her hand clenching tight on the railing. Her heart fluttered in her chest and she tried to make herself move.

Was she really considering this? She had no idea if he was actually attracted to her or just an irrepressible flirt. Yet something inside was telling her to take a shot with this man.

It was crazy. Something she'd never considered. Yet right now, at this moment, she was definitely considering it. If he was available...could she do it? Seduce a stranger. Have an anonymous fling, like something out of a blue movie on late-night cable?

She didn't know. All she knew was that the flight to Chicago was a short one, so she had to decide quickly. And as she put her foot on the bottom step and began to climb up, Amanda suddenly had to wonder if she was about to embark on the ride of her life.

Look for
PLAY WITH ME
by Leslie Kelly
Available February 2010

HARLEQUIN
Ambassadors

Want to share your passion for reading Harlequin® Books?

Become a Harlequin Ambassador!

Harlequin Ambassadors are a group of passionate and well-connected readers who are willing to share their joy of reading Harlequin® books with family and friends.

You'll be sent all the tools you need to spark great conversation, including free books!

All we ask is that you share the romance with your friends and family!

You'll also be invited to have a say in new book ideas and exchange opinions with women just like you!

To see if you qualify* to be a Harlequin Ambassador, please visit www.HarlequinAmbassadors.com.

*Please note that not everyone who applies to be a Harlequin Ambassador will qualify. For more information please visit www.HarlequinAmbassadors.com.

Thank you for your participation.

BAP09BPA

REQUEST YOUR FREE BOOKS!
2 FREE NOVELS PLUS 2 FREE GIFTS!

♣ HARLEQUIN®

American ★ Romance®

Love, Home & Happiness!

YES! Please send me 2 FREE Harlequin® American Romance® novels and my 2 FREE gifts (gifts are worth about $10). After receiving them, if I don't wish to receive any more books, I can return the shipping statement marked "cancel." If I don't cancel, I will receive 4 brand-new novels every month and be billed just $4.24 per book in the U.S. or $4.99 per book in Canada. That's a saving of close to 15% off the cover price! It's quite a bargain! Shipping and handling is just 50¢ per book in the U.S. and 75¢ per book in Canada.* I understand that accepting the 2 free books and gifts places me under no obligation to buy anything. I can always return a shipment and cancel at any time. Even if I never buy another book from Harlequin, the two free books and gifts are mine to keep forever.

154 HDN E4CC   354 HDN E4CN

Name _____ (PLEASE PRINT)

Address _____ Apt. #

City _____ State/Prov. _____ Zip/Postal Code

Signature (if under 18, a parent or guardian must sign)

Mail to the Harlequin Reader Service:
IN U.S.A.: P.O. Box 1867, Buffalo, NY 14240-1867
IN CANADA: P.O. Box 609, Fort Erie, Ontario L2A 5X3

Not valid for current subscribers to Harlequin® American Romance® books.

Want to try two free books from another line?
Call 1-800-873-8635 or visit www.morefreebooks.com.

* Terms and prices subject to change without notice. Prices do not include applicable taxes. N.Y. residents add applicable sales tax. Canadian residents will be charged applicable provincial taxes and GST. Offer not valid in Quebec. This offer is limited to one order per household. All orders subject to approval. Credit or debit balances in a customer's account(s) may be offset by any other outstanding balance owed by or to the customer. Please allow 4 to 6 weeks for delivery. Offer available while quantities last.

Your Privacy: Harlequin is committed to protecting your privacy. Our Privacy Policy is available online at www.eHarlequin.com or upon request from the Reader Service. From time to time we make our lists of customers available to reputable third parties who may have a product or service of interest to you. If you would prefer we not share your name and address, please check here. ☐

Help us get it right—We strive for accurate, respectful and relevant communications. To clarify or modify your communication preferences, visit us at www.ReaderService.com/consumerschoice.

HAR10

HARLEQUIN® *Blaze*™

*It all started
with a few naughty books....*

As a member of the Red Tote Book Club,
Carol Snow has been studying works of
classic erotic literature…but Carol doesn't
believe in love…or marriage. It's going to take
another kind of classic—Charles Dickens's
A Christmas Carol—and a little otherworldly
persuasion to convince her to go after her
own sexily ever after.

Cuddle up with

Her Sexy Valentine

by STEPHANIE BOND

Available February 2010

---

red-hot reads

www.eHarlequin.com

HB79526